LOVEY CHILDS:

A Philadelphian's Story

BOOKS BY JOHN O'HARA

LOVEY CHILDS

A Philadelphian's Story

A NOVEL BY

John O'Hara

HODDER AND STOUGHTON

Copyright © 1969 by John O'Hara
First Printed in Great Britain 1970

SBN 340 12891 7

Reproduced from the U.S. Edition by arrangement with
Random House, New York

Printed in Great Britain for Hodder and Stoughton Limited,
St. Paul's House, Warwick Lane, London, E.C.4, by
Compton Printing Ltd., London and Aylesbury

To ALBERT ERSKINE

LOVEY CHILDS:

A Philadelphian's Story

This is the story of Lovey Childs, of Philadelphia. In a certain world it would not be necessary to say "of Philadelphia"; the inhabitants of that world needed no more than her nickname, and that had always been the case from the time she was a little girl and not yet Lovey Childs. She began life as Charlotte Lewis, but Charlotte was such a majestic name for such a friendly, outgoing child that her immediate family, then her numerous cousins, and finally everyone else called her by the nickname her mother had given her at age three. In shops, on trains, she would fix her gaze on a stranger who interested her, and say, "I'm Lovey." There were not many men or women who refused to respond to her friendliness in kind. Other children have often said, "I'm Mary" and "I'm Helen," but when a sapphire-eyed child says "I'm Lovey" it can be taken as a self-appraisal, an invitation, or a statement of fact. In her childhood, when Lovey introduced herself to grownups they would at least smile, and she grew up in the belief that the grown-up world was a friendly place. She could hardly wait to become a member of that world, and she did all she could to hasten her entrance into it.

She liked to be in the company of adults, to imitate their speech and their manners, to earn their approval. Correspondingly she had a lack of interest in the lives of her contemporaries, and they in turn were cold to her. "You ought to play with children your own age," her mother would say. But whenever Mrs. Lewis invited other children to their house, Lovey would wander off and talk to Guy Glynn, the gardener, or to Walter Hughes, the chauffeur, or to one of the workmen who always seemed to be busy somewhere on the Lewis place. There were nearly always one or two carpenters or plumbers or housepainters on the place for Lovey to talk to, and it became increasingly difficult for Mrs. Lewis to find playmates for Lovey. "Well, she sees other children at school all day," said her father. "I was like

[4]

that, myself. Children my own age bored hell out of me."

"But you were a boy," said Mrs. Lewis. "I don't think it's nice for Lovey to be around those men so much. She picks up words that she doesn't know the meaning of, and you never know when she's going to come out with them. She says 'Damn it' all the time, but the ones I was thinking of are much worse."

"Still I don't think it does her any great harm. After all, she doesn't get home from school till four o'clock, and that doesn't give her much time to fraternize, I guess the word is. The men that come here are a pretty decent sort. Family men, most of them, with good jobs and so forth. I know most of them, and in many cases I knew their fathers. I don't have to tell *you*, Dorothy, if it's a question of foul language, Lovey's more liable to hear it from *our* friends than from Zigler the plumber or Stoner the carpenter. I give you Joe Fuller, or Celia Fuller for that matter."

"Yes, but that's just the point. I don't want Lovey to grow up talking like Celia. Celia doesn't even know she's saying those things any more."

"Well, what do you think we ought to do?"

"I wish I knew," said Dorothy Lewis.

"One thing I hope you don't do," said Billy Lewis.

"Don't forbid her to have her little chats with the work-men. She's only twelve, but very soon she'll grow out of her interest in men like Zigler and start taking an interest in boys. That's when the problem starts. Let's save our worrying till then."

"All right, but I hope you take a firmer stand than you're taking now," said Dorothy. "Because she's going to be an attractive young girl, and I'll need a lot of help from you."

She got no help from Billy Lewis. When Lovey was sixteen Billy Lewis broke his neck and died in the hunting field. All his friends said he should have known better than to try to get one more year out of that horse, a grey gelding that was the same age as Lovey, and known to be blind in one eye. But Billy Lewis had always been so knowledgeable about hunters (and little else) that if he insisted the horse was good for another season, who would have the nerve to argue with him? There was another factor that made the subject of the half-blind grey a delicate one: Billy himself was blind in one eye, a condition that had kept him out of the war and made blindness and the war topics to be avoided. Everybody liked Billy Lewis, but he seldom ventured outside his own circle of friends in the Radnor Hunt, the Philadelphia

Club, the Fish House, and The Rabbit. All the Lewis
money and all the skill of the Philadelphia specialists
could not restore the sight of his right eye, destroyed by
a pebble kicked up by Joe Fuller's horse when Billy and
Joe were eighteen years of age. Billy died almost but not
quite literally with his boots on; they cut off his boots
before taking him into the operating room at the hospital. But he never regained consciousness after his spill,
and someone remarked that at least Billy was spared the
knowledge of the mutilation of his boots. In Billy's scheme
of things a pair of twenty-five-year-old boots were price-
less. Someone at the hospital did remember to give Dorothy her husband's spurs, and someone who had been at
the scene of the accident picked Billy's crop off the
ground and left it at the Lewis house.

Dorothy went into mourning of a kind: as soon as the
last visitor left her house after the funeral she opened
a bottle and filled a silver stirrup cup with gin. The
cup was a trophy, made of sterling and decorated with
a fox-head. She drank the gin ceremonially, silently
toasting a portrait of Billy Lewis in scarlet evening
coat and white tie which hung above the fireplace in
his den. She then sat down and lit a cigarette and for
the next few hours she sat in the big leather chair,

drinking the gin and smoking cigarettes until she fell asleep. No one disturbed her. At ten o'clock Lovey tapped lightly on the door of the den, opened it, saw her mother sprawled in the chair, covered her with a comforter, and went to her own room. She had never before seen her mother drunk, *that* drunk, but her father had often been in a condition that he described as "plastered to the hat," and at such times he was unfailingly generous, slightly sentimental, and nicely silly. If her mother wanted to get drunk on this sad day, Lovey did not mind having dinner alone and going to bed without a goodnight kiss. Older people got drunk when they were having a good time and when they were sad, and often they turned their sadness into a good time and their good time into sadness. Her mother, for example, came upstairs around midnight singing "A-hunting we will go, a hunting we will go," said Lovey, watching her through a partly opened door, saw that she was wearing Billy's spurs like bracelets and waving her hands in time to her song.

The next day Lovey went back to school in Virginia, to a place and a way of life that she loathed. There was a strong emphasis on horsemanship at the school, but since Lovey was her father's daughter she had been riding almost since she could walk, and horsemanship had become second nature to her. The compliments she received on her riding affected her not at all; it was like being praised for brushing your teeth. Some girls at the school hated riding, were terrified of it; others liked nothing about the school but the riding. But with Lovey, riding belonged to childhood and so did everything else at the school. Now that she was back from the maturing experience of her father's funeral—the older people had never seemed older—she made a rather mature decision: she would first try persuasion, and if that did not work, she would use other means to get her mother to take her out of the school.

Persuasion failed, as she knew it would, and in a sense she welcomed the failure. It became necessary for her to act upon her decision. Accordingly, she borrowed small sums from various girls until she had $30, and one morning she packed a small bag, waited until the other girls were in classrooms, sent for a taxi, and boldly rode to the railway station and took the train to Washington.

She got home late in the afternoon, and her mother was waiting for her. "Lovey, why did you do it?" said Dorothy. "I didn't realize you were so unhappy there. Neither did Miss Brandon. She telephoned me immediately."

"That taxi driver is a spy. Everybody knows that,"

said Lovey. "But I didn't care. I'm here, and I'm not going back."

"No, I don't suppose you are. Miss Brandon's very displeased, to say the least. The first time in the history of the school that a girl actually carried out a threat to run away."

"Well, fancy that. They all talk about it, but I was the first one to do it. Good for me."

"Now just a minute, young lady. Just—a—minute."

"Mummy, I know what you're going to say," said Lovey.

"No you don't, because I don't know myself. At least I don't know where to start. *Why* didn't you like the school?"

"Because I didn't. They treated us like children in kindergarten. They wanted us to behave like young ladies, young ladies, young ladies, but they made us wear those awful clothes and the only privacy we ever get is in the bathroom. Even there they accidentally on purpose open the door to see what you're doing."

"There are reasons for that," said Dorothy.

"Oh, come on, Mummy, don't *you* talk to me like a child."

"What else are you, if you're not a child?"

"Biologically, I'm a woman. I could have a baby."

"Well, I hope you're not."

"I'm not, but I could. I know all about that, too."

"Do you? From experience?"

"No. Not yet. But we're all built the same—women, girls. Unfortunately. Some of the girls at school should have been built like boys. They pretended they were."

"Oh, was that the trouble? Did one of those girls— get too friendly?"

"That wasn't what I meant. What I meant was that if one of the girls *had* been built like a boy, she could have done what boys do, and then they wouldn't have talked about it so much. That was the trouble. They pretended to know so much and they didn't know a damn thing."

"Exactly, and that's why they had to treat you like children."

"Maybe that was all right for the rest of them, but I couldn't stand it any longer. I'm not a child. I've been having the bloody nuisance for four years."

"Is that what they call it?"

"It's what I call it. I don't care what anyone else calls it."

"You've always been in such a hurry to grow up.

Well, that's part of it. Growing up isn't the heaven you think it is."

"I never thought it was heaven, but being a child is so artificial. People *talk* differently to you, and all the rest of it. You're just as much of a human being as they are, but just because you're younger—and besides, that awful nickname, Lovey."

"They called you Lottie at school. Did you like that better?"

"No, one's as bad as the other," said Lovey.

"You were given the name Charlotte because your father's aunt was named Charlotte and all her money went to him. I called you Lovey because you were such a darling, lovable baby, and then your father took it up and everybody else. But now the question is, where does our Lovey go to continue her education? You have a lot to learn, in more ways than one. And one of them is, you can't just walk away from something because it bores you. Incidentally, it was your father that picked Miss Brandon's, I didn't."

"That reminds me. Are you going to keep the horses?" said Lovey.

"As long as you'll ride them, yes."

"Then sell them. I don't care if I never ride another horse as long as I live."

"We ought to keep *one*. The expense isn't very great, and if you're going to be here for the next few years, time will weigh very heavily on your hands."

"Am I going to stay here the next few years?"

"There's no use sending you to another boarding-school."

"Ah, thank you, Mummy. You are sweet, you really are," said Lovey. "I don't have to go away to boarding-school? You mean it?"

"Of course I mean it. I only hope it turns out to be the right decision. There must be one of the schools near here that will take you."

"Mummy, it won't be so difficult. Billy Lewis's daughter. We don't have to pretend to each other. F. Willingham Lewis—even Miss Brandon was impressed by Daddy. The headmistress of a school being impressed by a horseman. That was the trouble with that place. It was more a stable than a school."

"Well, we'll see if you do better at a more educational institution," said Dorothy.

"Be fair, Mummy. Did I ever flunk anything at Miss Brandon's?"

"No. But I never said you weren't bright," said Dorothy. "Go on upstairs and unpack and get ready for dinner. I have to go over to Mrs. Fuller's for a little while."

"Are you going to tell her about me?" said Lovey.

"Why not? Everybody's going to know in a few days."

"Oh, I want her to know. I want everybody to know. The sooner the better is how I look at it."

"Why?"

"Because it is," said Lovey. "It is, you know. The sooner the better. 'Lovey Lewis ran away from school. My goodness!' If I'm old enough to run away from school, I'm old enough to do a lot of other things. Mrs. Fuller's going to be disappointed, though. She's not going to believe I just got sick of it. She's going to be sure I'm knocked up—"

"Oh, Lovey, that's not fair to Mrs. Fuller," said Dorothy. "And it's not a nice expression to use, either."

"It's what she'd say," said Lovey.

"Why don't you like Mrs. Fuller?"

"Because she cried too much at Daddy's funeral. She didn't like Daddy and Daddy didn't like her, but she was just trying to attract attention. She grabbed hold of me and said, 'Oh, you poor, dear child, what are you going to do?' I wanted to slap her."

"When was that?" said Dorothy.

"When they were all standing around having drinks, here, after we came back from the church."

"You mustn't be so critical, Lovey. It's very unbecoming at your age."

"I'd rather be critical than hypocritical. As soon as she saw nobody was paying any attention to her, she left me and went and tried to flirt with Mr. Geddes. A person must be pretty hard up when they have to flirt with Mr. Geddes. And what was *he* doing at Daddy's funeral? Daddy didn't like him, either."

"There again, you're being so critical. Not all of those people came because they were friends of your father's. Some of them were there because they wanted to comfort *me*."

"They could have done that some other time," said Lovey. "And I'm sure some of them were there because Daddy was F. Willingham Lewis."

"You seem to have that on the brain, today. Why, I wonder?"

"Because that awful school was full of social climbers, and Miss Brandon was the worst. You have no idea."

"I've heard her called a snob, but never a social climber. I understand the Brandons go back to time immemorial. In fact, your father said that Miss Brandon was the first one in her line that wasn't a general. Well, I hear the car."

"I'm going out and say hello to Walter," said Lovey.

"Oh, I'm afraid it isn't Walter any more," said Dorothy. "I had to let him go."

"Mummy, you didn't!"

"But I did. I haven't got time to explain it now."

"Did you sack him, or did he give notice?"

"Six of one and half a dozen of the other. Later," said Dorothy. "I should be home before seven."

Lovey went to the sitting-room window and saw that the car was the same, the big black Pierce-Arrow limousine that her father would not get rid of. But now instead of Walter Hughes to close the door there was a younger man in a new grey livery and new puttees, and if he did not get a good look at her mother's legs, Lovey did. The man closed the door and got behind the wheel, and Lovey saw her mother smile and speak to him with unmistakable pleasure. She had never seen her mother smile at Walter Hughes, and she had never seen Walter Hughes smile at her. It was horrible to see her mother so unguardedly stimulated by the nearness of this new man, horrible to see with her own eyes and in her own family this evidence of a trite situation that she had never quite believed could be true—the rich woman, the young chauffeur. And he was young, certainly younger than her mother; thirty, thirty-five, that age. The great lumbering limousine turned into Wissahickon Lane and was out of sight. It was horrible, sickening to be sure that her mother had deliberately flashed her legs at the chauffeur and was in such a short time on chatty terms with him. Suddenly the adventure of running home from school was spoiled for Lovey. The house was too big, the empty chairs and sofas too big, the world too wide, her father too dead, her mother too deceitful.

She had eaten a ham sandwich while changing trains in the Washington station, but it was not a very good ham sandwich, and she was hungry again. She went back to the kitchen and found a tea party in progress: the cook, the parlormaid, the chambermaid, and the gardener. "Sorry to intrude," said Lovey. "But I'm starving." She guessed from their abrupt silence that they had been discussing her and her return. "Were you talking about *me?*"

"Suppose we were? Is there a law against that?" said Mary Carmody, the cook. "It took an empty stomach to bring you here and say hello, did it?"

"Oh, you know better than that," said Lovey. "Hello, Guy. How are your kidneys?"

"Now never you mind about my kidneys," said the gardener.

"Hello, Ellen. I've already spoken to you, Kitty. By

the way, I noticed a new chauffeur. When did Walter leave?"

"This good while," said Mary. "Two-three weeks after the funeral, would you say, Ellen?"

"Around there somewhere," said the chambermaid.

"Where's Walter? Has he got a job?" said Lovey.

"Not the last I heard," said Mary.

"He got a year's pay," said Guy. "He can look around. He can pick and choose."

"Walter's all right. You don't have to worry about him," said Ellen.

"Where is he living?" said Lovey.

"In the city, the last I heard," said Mary. "He took a room."

"What else is new?" said Lovey.

"What else is new? Not much. We're all here, except Walter," said Mary.

"I guess you knew Gypsy died," said Guy.

"*She* would of told her that," said Mary.

"My mother? No, she didn't tell me," said Lovey. "How did Gypsy die?"

"The distemper, I guess," said Guy. "She was getting on anyhow. Them big dogs don't last as long as the littler ones."

"Some of them do," said Ellen. "We had a—"

"She died of a broken heart," said Mary.

"That's what I think, too," said Kitty. "Every time I went in the den, there she was, lying underneath the table like she was hiding. She wouldn't hardly look up when you came in the room."

"She knew everybody's footsteps, that's why. She knew *he* wasn't coming," said Mary.

"Once they lose the will to live, it's better to put them out of their misery," said Ellen.

"Did Guy have to shoot her?" said Lovey.

"No, she just died," said Guy. "I don't think I would of had the heart to shoot her. Next to your father I guess I was fonder of her than anyone else, although in the beginning she did give me a lot of trouble. I just hope your mother don't go and get another wolfhound."

"She won't," said Mary. "I'd be surprised if we ever had another dog in this house."

"Well, I hope it isn't a wolfhound. They can make a lot of extra work, one way or the other," said Kitty.

"Especially the other, if you know what I mean," said Ellen.

"Gypsy was house-broke," said Kitty.

"There's none of them house-broke if you don't leave them out at the proper time," said Ellen.

"I loved Gypsy," said Lovey.

"Oh, you couldn't help loving her," said Kitty. "But such a big dog oughtn't to be in the house so much."

"Or in my rose-garden," said Guy. "It took me near a year to learn her to stay out of that one particular spot. I'd get her so she knew better and then F. W. would come down to talk to me about something or other, and she'd be trailing right along with him. Finally I had to tell him, I said if he wanted roses growing in my garden, to keep Gypsy out of there."

"What did Daddy say? He cared more about Gypsy than he did about roses," said Lovey.

"Maybe he did, but he kept her out of there. I wasn't giving orders, getting out of my place, but if you put something to him in the right way, he'd listen to reason."

"That he would," said Mary. "He never came past that pantry door without knocking. The kitchen was my territory, he used to say."

"But if you ever went in his den without knocking he'd give you hail-Columbia," said Kitty.

"I know why that was," said Mary. "He used to sit there in the dark with his glass eye out. He didn't want anybody to see him with it out. He was very particular about that."

"In the morning, too," said Ellen. "You couldn't bring him his coffee till he had his eye in."

"Did you decide what you wanted to eat?" said Mary.

"Nothing, thanks," said Lovey.

"It's a wonder she has any appetite after this conversation," said Kitty.

"You're right, Kitty," said Lovey. "Sick dogs and glass eyes. Excuse *me*."

"Now don't take it out on us because you were sent home from school," said Mary. "We're all sorry you had to be punished, but don't turn around and punish us. We have enough to put up with—"

"Mary, Mary," said Kitty.

"Don't Mary-Mary me," said Mary.

"Discretion is the better part of value, I always heard," said Guy.

"Now what are you all talking about?" said Lovey. "You weren't talking about me when I came in. You were gossiping about my mother."

"Ah, now don't let's fly off the handle," said Guy. "You don't want to go imagining things."

"You'll only upset yourself, imagining such things," said Ellen.

Lovey left them and went to her room. Her bed was stripped down to the mattress and a dust-cover, the windows closed tight, in the bathroom there was no soap on the washstand or in the wall receptacle above the tub, and when she turned the water on it came out spitting and rusty. She had run away from nothing to nothing and no one, and at this moment, at Miss Brandon's, a hundred chattering, hungry girls were on their way to supper. Thursday. They always had pork chops and apple sauce for Thursday supper. The apple sauce was sprinkled with cinnamon.

The new school had a Bryn Mawr address, but the headmistress was always scrupulous about reminding parents from the Middle West that Hathaway did not have and did not claim any official connection with the college. "We are actually older than Bryn Mawr College," she would say. "We began in 1882 as Bishop Hathaway's Seminary for Young Ladies, named after old Bishop John Matthew Hathaway, naturally. The school was destroyed by fire in 1895 and wasn't reopened until 1902, the year I came here. They decided then to change the name to Hathaway Hall and to admit girls from other states, which of course meant that we'd be a boarding-school. We've had girls from as far away as China and from every state in the Union except Utah and Nevada. One rather unique feature of our enrollment is that we always have at least six or eight girls whose fathers are army officers, and those girls of course are very well traveled. We wanted to get away from the old idea of taking girls from a few of the Eastern States. About one-third of our girls come from the Philadelphia area, the day students, but we never let the proportion of day scholars exceed that number. Some of our girls naturally don't intend to go on to college, but for those who do we have the preparatory course, and we're rather proud of our record in that respect. We've had some at Bryn Mawr, and others at Smith, Vassar, Goucher, Wellesley, Wilson—almost every prominent women's college. About half of our girls take the college preparatory courses, but we're still putting more emphasis on retaining our standing as a finishing school. One year we had eight alumnae who were presidents of their local chapters of the Junior League. I think that's quite remarkable, and is an indication of the high type of girl we take at Hathaway as well as the education and training we offer. We're not an expensive school, and don't pretend to be. But we have to turn away any number of girls from wealthy homes because we want to maintain our standards. We're not affiliated with any religious denomination, but I'd say that more than ninety percent of our girls come from Episcopalian or Presbyterian families."

Ida Van Fleet Roberts could make this speech in her sleep, but it was not necessary to repeat it in the case of Charlotte Willingham Lewis. A telephone call from Dorothy Lewis to Joe Fuller was followed by a telephone call from Joe Fuller to Ida Van Fleet Roberts, and Lovey was admitted to Hathaway Hall. Joe Fuller was a trustee of Hathaway, and in matters of this kind he knew just what to do. You *asked* Ida Roberts to take Lovey Lewis, but you left no doubt in Ida's mind that you were *telling* her. "Don't you think I ought to have an interview with the girl?" said Ida.

"Sure," said Joe Fuller. "But this isn't some epileptic nigger kid. She's the daughter of my best friend, Billy Lewis. Got killed in a hunting accident a couple of months ago. F. Willingham Lewis. You've lived around here long enough to know who he was."

Ida Roberts restrained herself from telling Joe Fuller that he was a trustee because F. Willingham Lewis had turned it down. "Oh, yes, I know who they are," she said. "Well, if you'll vouch for her, and Mollie Brandon gives us a good report, we'll make room for her."

"Mollie Brandon my foot, Ida," said Joe Fuller. "This is Philadelphia, not Virginia."

On the morning of the interview Lovey and Dorothy Lewis arrived at Hathaway Hall in the black Pierce-Arrow ten minutes early. They were greeted by Ida Van Fleet Roberts as the school bell struck the hour. "Good morning, Mrs. Lewis, and good morning, Charlotte. Do come in and take a seat. This is really what the boys call football weather, isn't it? It's too bad they didn't have it last week for the Penn-Cornell game. The field was so squishy."

"Oh, did you go?" said Dorothy.

"Never miss it. My brother would disown me, although we have so much going on at Hathaway on Thanksgiving that I can never stay for the second half. Your husband went to Penn, too, I believe?"

"Yes. To St. Bartholomew's and then to Penn," said Dorothy.

"Charlotte, have you been to many football games?"

"I beg your pardon?" said Lovey.

"She's not used to being called Charlotte," said Dorothy. "She's always been known by a nickname that I gave her. Lovey. She doesn't like it very much, but the Philadelphia girls here at school will call her that."

"Well, of course I don't use the girls' nicknames, not even Kitty for Katharine," said Ida Van Fleet Roberts.

"It smacks of over-familiarity and possible favoritism. My friend Miss Brandon spoke of you as Lottie."

"I like Charlotte better than Lottie," said Lovey.

"Charlotte is a pretty name, but I'm inclined to agree with you about Lottie," said Ida Van Fleet Roberts. "Tell me, what are your favorite subjects? You had fairly good marks at Miss Brandon's but marks don't always tell the whole story."

"English, I guess," said Lovey. "It was the easiest."

Ida Roberts smiled at Dorothy Lewis. "A frank answer," said Ida Roberts. "When I was in college my favorite subject was higher algebra, but I was never able to get more than an eighty-five in it."

"Lovey was good in algebra, weren't you, dear?"

"Pretty good," said Lovey.

"Well, now what about extra-curricular activities? Sports, for instance? I'm sure you ride well. We have an arrangement with a local stable for girls who take riding, and several of our girls board their own horses there."

"She practically grew up in the saddle," said Dorothy.

"Have you a-hunting gone, Charlotte?" said Ida Roberts.

"Yes," said Lovey.

"Her father—" said Dorothy.

"Yes, I know, Mrs. Lewis. But I wanted to see how Charlotte would react to the subject. We have to use psychology, you know. We're learning new methods all the time, in education. Some of them I'm not prepared to accept, but some of them can be helpful. I had to know whether Charlotte had recovered from her father's unfortunate accident. And I believe she has."

"I see," said Dorothy.

"Yes, I think Charlotte is what we call a well-adjusted girl," said Ida Roberts. "I wish I could ask you to stay for lunch, but I have a previous engagement at the Acorn Club, something I can't break. However, Miss King will show you around. She's my assistant. She'll introduce you to our teachers and tell you all about uniforms and so forth. I'd like Charlotte to be here for assembly tomorrow at eight-forty-five. She can wear what she has on now till her uniforms are fitted."

Ida Van Fleet Roberts rose, concluding the interview, and Lovey and Dorothy were asked to wait in Miss King's office. For a moment they were alone. "Well, what did you think?" said Dorothy.

"I guess I can't get in any place else," said Lovey.

"And at least you'll be living at home," said Dorothy. "What did you think of Miss Roberts?"

"Miss Brandon, only worse," said Lovey.

"Try to make the best of it till next year. And anyway, you may change your mind," said Dorothy.

At Hathaway the Philadelphia girls were for the most part daughters of men and women who were acquainted with Dorothy and Billy Lewis. The boarders were on the whole children of men and women a cut or two below the Philadelphia parents, a fact which Lovey knew as well as it could be known without actually seeing the parents. At Miss Brandon's there had been a girl called Kitty Gotrocks, the granddaughter of the tenth or twelfth wealthiest man in the United States, so rich that instead of donating a dormitory to a university, he founded an entirely new college. Kitty's parents chose to live in New York, but the Gotrocks name—actually the old man's name was Jacob Morland—was so universally associated with the steel industry that no matter where the Morlands lived, they were Pittsburghers. Kitty Gotrocks was at Miss Brandon's for one reason and one reason only: to get her ready for her coming-out party, an event for which she was preparing as zealously as her mother. There were no poor girls at Miss Brandon's, but even the richest of them were offering suggestions to make Kitty's party the most memorable in the history of the United States. In time the suggestions became frivolous and fantastic, and Kitty became pathetic in her blind ignorance of the fact that the girls were putting her on. A girl from Boston suggested to Kitty that her family take over the entire Ritz-Carlton hotel to make it a truly private party. Two weeks later Kitty regretfully informed her Boston friend that the Ritz management was unable (or unwilling) to make the necessary arrangements with the hotel's permanent residents. But the Boston girl's next suggestion—that the complete cast of the Ziegfeld Follies be engaged for the entertainment interval—was acted upon favorably. No Kitty Gotrocks was at Hathaway, but Hathaway was not Miss Brandon's, and among the boarders Lovey soon discovered a dozen girls who had the same eagerness to spend their fathers', or grandfathers', money. The Hathaway girls' parties were going to be held at hotels with German names and country clubs with Indian names, in cities that Lovey never expected to visit that were inhabited by boys who were invariably identified by the Greek letters of their fraternities ("What is a Beta from Ann Arbor? What does he bait?" asked Lovey in her ignorance). To Lovey it was a revelation that less than ten miles from her house was a colony of girls who had never heard of the Fish House or the City Troop, and who could hardly wait to get back to the prairies. They were like a religious cult, exiled to the very small corner of Pennsylvania that to her was home. They were like immobilized gypsies, waiting to take the train at Paoli. They were rather like the girls she had so recently left at Miss Brandon's, and like the girls at Miss Brandon's they offered her nothing she wanted to keep.

The Christmas vacation was near, and in her weeks at Hathaway Lovey had yet to meet a girl she could like. The measure was that she had met a few whom she disliked less than the others. The near-hysteria among the boarders as their departure time was measurable in hours was irritating. Her status as the newest girl in the school had kept her subdued, but two days before vacation she lost patience. In the dining hall, at lunch, an ebullient girl from Minnesota, seventeen years old and condescending to everyone younger, ostentatiously took a letter out of her middy-blouse pocket and waved it in the air. "Don't be surprised, you poor unsophisticated pieces of humanity, if you don't see me after Christmas. Supper tonight, breakfast tomorrow, lunch tomorrow, supper tomorrow, breakfast and lunch the next day. That's how many? Six more meals to eat here, and just don't you be surprised if someone else is sitting here on the sixth of January instead of me."

"You going to elope, Karen?" said a girl.

Karen waved the letter. "Ask me no questions, I'll tell you no lies."

"Is it the Phi Gam?" said the girl.

"Good grief, no. That's ancient history. This one's a Zete. You remember I told you about the Zete from Cornell? This is the one. The one and only."

"The lucky Phi Gam," said Lovey.

"Another country heard from. I thought you didn't know what a Phi Gam was," said Karen.

"I didn't before I had to listen to you every day," said Lovey.

"Is that so? I just like to know why you had to leave Miss Brandon's in such a hurry. Tell us that, Miss Charlotte, rhymes with harlot. I'll find out when I get home. I know a girl at Brandon's, and I'll get the real story from her. Believe you me, it takes a lot to get you shipped home from that stuck-up place."

The faculty member who usually sat at the head of the table was absent, and by custom the senior at the table was left in charge. At the moment the senior girl was Karen.

"May I be excused?" said Lovey.

"No, you may not," said Karen. "I have a few more things to say to you, Miss Philadelphia Society."

"Go ahead. You're a vulgar, silly girl anyway," said

Lovey. "Nothing you could possibly say would affect me in the slightest, not the slightest."

"I wouldn't waste my breath," said Karen. She rose and left.

The girl on Lovey's right said, "You just made a bad enemy. She can be mean."

"What if she can?" said Lovey. "Anyway, she's not coming back—she says."

"She says, but she wasn't coming back in September, either. She thinks every boy wants to marry her. She has marriage on the bean. She wants to be the first girl in her class to get married."

"I pity the poor boy," said Lovey.

"Well, so do I, but I'm not going to say that to Karen. She's a suck."

"What?"

"She likes to be in good with the faculty, so she tattles on everybody. Of course she's not the only one, unfortunately." The girl was Marcy Bancroft, daughter of an army officer now stationed in the Canal Zone. She was a class ahead of Lovey and destined for Vassar. Because of their schedules Marcy and Lovey saw each other only at lunch and in the gymnasium, and this was their first unstilted conversation.

"Well, I'm not afraid of her," said Lovey.

"All the same, she can make trouble for you, and will if she gets the chance," said Marcy Bancroft.

"She can't make trouble for you. You're on the honor roll."

"I have to be. I'm on scholarship. If you're on scholarship you have to stay out of trouble," said Marcy.

"We're not supposed to know who is on scholarship, are we?" said Lovey. "I knew at Miss Brandon's, but that was because everybody was rich there except the girls on scholarship. At least that's the way we figured it out. Two girls, their fathers were ministers. But your father is an army officer."

"He couldn't afford a school like this on captain's pay. I don't mind admitting I'm on scholarship, and everybody could guess. I couldn't go home for Christmas even if there was time."

"Where *are* you going?" said Lovey.

"West Point," said Marcy.

"You going to be there the whole vacation?"

"No. I'll be there Christmas Eve and Christmas Day and another two days. My godfather and godmother are there, but then they have to go someplace, so I come back here."

"Would you like to come and stay at my house?"

"I wasn't hinting, Lovey. When you're an army brat you get used to different living. I haven't been with my family for Christmas since I was thirteen. I like going to West Point. Last year my godmother took me to New York and we stayed at the Astor House and saw a matinee and did some shopping. We get discounts at all the good stores. My father's saving up all his leave for next summer."

"Where will you go then?"

"To my uncle's ranch in Nebraska. I haven't been there since Daddy was at Riley. That's in Kansas."

"Kansas. Nebraska. You're talking about places I've never been near," said Lovey.

"It gets terribly hot at the ranch, but everywhere I've ever lived it was hot. Except Schofield, we always had a breeze there. That's in the Hawaiian Islands. We're hoping my father's sent to West Point the year after next. That's just across the river, you know, from Vassar, where I'll be. But the army never lets you know till the last minute. He *could* be sent to Alaska, and I'd hate that. He was a colonel during the war but then he had to go back to first lieutenant, and he has quite a few classmates that still haven't made captain. It's even worse in the navy, and if you get sea duty your wife can't be with you. I'd never marry an Annapolis man. They're gone for months at a time."

"Would you marry an army officer?" said Lovey.

"Well, not before I finish college," said Marcy. "They want me to get a degree, and they've made a lot of sacrifices for my education. When my grandmother dies my mother will inherit *some* money, but all my father will have is his pension. He could teach math at some college. He's an artillery officer, and they're sharks at math. But I guess there isn't much difference between an officer's pay and a math professor's. How did I get started on all this? Talking about my scholarship, I guess. If I don't get a scholarship I can't go to Vassar, and that's why I have to stay on the honor roll here. They look into your past record before they give you a scholarship at Vassar, believe me. Wouldn't it be awful if I fell in love and the boy wanted me to elope—I mean really wanted me to, not an imaginary elopement like Karen's."

"It'd be all right if he was terribly rich," said Lovey.

"Don't *say* that! The number of times I've thought how wonderful it would be if some Princeton millionaire would give my father a million dollars for his consent. 'Captain Bancroft, this small token of my—' Uh-uh. There's the bell!"

"Thank you, Marcy," said Lovey.

"For what?" said Marcy.

"Oh—just thank you," said Lovey.

That evening at dinner Dorothy asked the routine question: "How did it go in school today?"

"Much better."

"Good. Why?" said Dorothy.

"Mummy, is it all right if I invite a girl to spend some of her Christmas vacation here? Her name is Marcy Bancroft."

"Have the Bancrofts got a daughter at Hathaway? I used to know Cyril and Daphne Bancroft when your father had the cottage in Aiken. But I don't remember a daughter."

"I don't think Marcy is any relation. Her father is an officer in the army, down at the Panama Canal."

"Then it isn't the same Bancrofts. Cyril Bancroft was usually so intoxicated that he used to fall out of his buckboard at least once a week. Fortunately he had an old nag that never went faster than a walk, and nothing serious ever happened. Daphne was always known behind her back as Daffy. Where does your friend come from?"

"I think from Nebraska."

"And her father is a general?"

"No, a captain," said Marcy.

"Well, I don't know why we can't have her for a few days. We're still in mourning, don't forget, so there won't be any entertaining. You could have a skating party, if the pond freezes. Or a small theater party. Take your friend in to a matinee. We'll see what's playing. Al Jolson was here, although I don't know if he still is. Does she ride? I'm sure she must if her father's in the army."

"I guess she rides, yes," said Lovey.

"It seems to me you don't know very much about her."

"I don't, but I like her better than any other girl at school, and she has to spend Christmas with her godfather and godmother at West Point."

"All right. Do I have to write a letter to Miss Roberts, or what?"

"I don't even know if Marcy will come. I haven't said anything to her, at least I haven't actually invited her. But I will tomorrow, if I may."

"By all means, then we can cook up something in the way of entertainment, on a suitable scale," said Dorothy.

The school was more than happy to grant permission to Marcy Bancroft for a four-day visit to Mrs. F. Willingham Lewis. It was of course too late for an exchange of letters with Marcy's parents, but Captain and Mrs. Ban-croft would surely be grateful to know that their daughter was being entertained in one of the representative Main Line homes. Miss Ida Van Fleet Roberts would take full responsibility for the change in plans.

Marcy arrived at the North Philadelphia station and was met by Lovey with the black Pierce-Arrow and the chauffeur Louis. "Did you have a good time at West Point?" said Lovey.

"Yes. It's changed in a year, or maybe I have. I guess I have. West Point doesn't change," said Marcy. "Hearing bugle calls again—I don't know."

"I don't think you did have a very good time. You sound depressed," said Lovey.

"I'd forgotten how Christmas always affects me. I'm glad it's over and past," said Marcy.

"Well, at least you won't hear any bugle calls at our house. Not even a hunting horn, with this snow. You did tell me you like skating, didn't you? Tomorrow we're having a skating party, all young people, then a sort of high tea. Nothing today. Mother thought you'd like a rest after West Point."

"I brought my skates. We skated at West Point," said Marcy.

"Mother will be home when we get there. She's looking forward to your visit. This is our first Christmas without Daddy, and it was pretty gloomy for both of us. He always celebrated Christmas in true Dickens fashion. Even a roast pig with an apple in its mouth, one year. It was a great disappointment when there wasn't enough snow to go calling on the neighbors in a sleigh."

"Yes, we went on a sleigh ride at The Point," said Marcy. "Oh, I had a good time, but I always think I'm not going to miss my family and then I do. Is this your house?"

"It's the porter's lodge. We live at the end of the lane."

"That big house?" said Marcy.

"That big house."

"And all this ground is yours?" said Marcy.

"There was more when my grandfather was alive. Daddy had to sell I don't know how many acres, for taxes. And Mummy will probably have to sell some more. That's all I hear, is how much we're going to sell, what we're going to have to give up. But Mummy says all her friends are in the same boat, or will be. Somebody dies and you inherit something, but then you have to find some way to pay the taxes. When Grandpa was alive

Mummy said they had thirty-five people working on the place, but I don't remember that. I was only two or three when he died. Grandpa had a house in Palm Beach, and one in Aiken, and one at Bar Harbor and a house on Delancey Street. One by one Daddy got rid of them all except this. Daddy never worked. Never held a job in his life and was determined that he never would have one. He used to say that there'll always be enough to live the way he liked to live, so why work? But that didn't keep him from putting money in the stock market, and he wasn't very lucky at that." Lovey looked to the right and left at the snow-covered lawns. "I know I won't have all this when I get older, but it'll be nice to look back on," she said.

Dorothy Lewis poured tea for the girls, dressed in a black lace costume that was both peignoir and frock, loose and cut low at the neck. "I'm going out to dinner and leave you two girls to yourselves. If you're still up when I get home I'll stop in to say goodnight," she said.

"Where are you having dinner?" said Lovey.

"The Williamses'," said Dorothy. "It's not a party. Just the Williamses and Mr. and Mrs. Fuller and I, and maybe Mr. Evans. It's the only chance we'll get to talk to Mr. Evans before he goes abroad. Mr. Williams and Mr.

Fuller think he might want to buy a piece of the land on Willingham Road. We hope he does."

"I was just telling Marcy about that, how much smaller this place is getting to be," said Lovey.

"Well, the Willingham Road land is nothing but a burden," said Dorothy. "Let's show Marcy her room and then I'll have to change."

For a brief moment mother and daughter were together in Dorothy's bedroom. "How did you like Marcy?" said Lovey.

"Adorable-looking, with those enormous brown eyes. But rather subdued. Is she always that way?" said Dorothy.

"She's .tired, and I don't think she had a very good time at West Point," said Lovey. "An attack of homesickness."

"Don't sit up talking. Let her get a good night's rest," said Dorothy.

"But you did like her?" said Lovey.

"She's rather fascinating, the way she follows every word and taking it all in. Yes, I like her," said Dorothy.

It was nearly midnight when Dorothy got home, looked in on Lovey and heard her deep breathing. From there she went to Marcy's room and opened the door. "It's all right, Mrs. Lewis. I'm awake," said Marcy.

"Oh, you must try to go to sleep, Marcy. It's nearly twelve o'clock. Goodnight," said Dorothy. She closed the door and went to her room, ran a tub, took a bath, and got into bed with a long legal paper that Williams and Fuller had asked her to read. It was hard reading, so full of repeated legal phrases and long sentences that twice she had to begin all over again. She put the paper on the night table to be read in the morning, and there was a light knock on the door, and Marcy's voice. "May I come in?"

"I'm in bed, Marcy," said Dorothy.

The door opened and the girl entered and stood at the side of the bed. "Will you let me get in bed with you for a little while?" said Marcy.

"Well—for just a minute. It's awfully late," said Dorothy. "Did you have a nightmare?"

"A sort of one," said the girl. She got into bed and lay her head on Dorothy's breast and Dorothy put her hand on the top of the girl's head. So they lay for a long minute, and the girl put her hand on Dorothy's other breast. The hand was heavy and made for some discomfort, but Dorothy left it there and said nothing. Then in a little while the breast was being fondled and Dorothy knew that this was the moment to send the girl back to her room. But she could not say the words and the

fondling continued. Now the girl pulled down the nightgown enough to bare the nipples and put her mouth
over one.

"Do you know what you're doing, Marcy?" said
Dorothy.

The girl nodded but did not speak.

"I shouldn't let you do that," said Dorothy. But she
could not harden her voice. "Marcy, this is very wrong,"
said Dorothy. Wrong, but she knew that the girl knew
that Dorothy was not ready to make her stop. The girl's
hand moved downward halfway down her belly and
stayed there, gently touching the skin with her fingertips,
so gently that in her tension Dorothy could scarcely feel
the touch until the hand made a crown over her hair.
This was the last chance to stop, and Dorothy knew that
nothing on earth could make her want the girl to stop.
Then the girl's finger was inside her and nothing could
ever change that fact. All the rest was innocuous fondling. Now the girl knelt on the bed and quickly pulled
her nightgown over her head and dropped it on the floor.
Dorothy sat up and took off her nightgown. Woman and
girl looked at each other, saying nothing, breaking the
stare that held their eyes only to look admiringly at each
other's body. Now Dorothy reached out and put her hands

on the girl's breasts and the girl smiled. Dorothy's hands
crept up to the girl's shoulders and over them and down
her back, and drew the girl to her until woman and girl
were in close embrace, breasts against breasts and belly
on belly. "You want me to kiss you," said the girl.

Dorothy nodded.

"Say 'Please, kiss me,'" said the girl.

"Please kiss me, Marcy."

"Will you promise to kiss me?" said Marcy.

"I promise," said the woman. She opened her legs and
the girl kissed her, and then the woman kissed the girl.
They lay in each other's arms for a long time, touching
each other everywhere.

"I know what you're thinking," said the girl.

"A thousand things. What?" said the woman.

"Do I do this to Lovey? The answer is no," said the
girl.

"No, I didn't think you did. But why me?"

"Because you're a woman, and a lady," said the girl.

"You thought I'd be experienced, and I wouldn't tell
anybody. Is that it?"

"Just about," said the girl.

"But how did you know I would?" said the woman.

"I always know."

"You've done this with a lot of women?"

"No, not many. I can't with the girls at school, because I'm on a scholarship and I'd be shipped home. I've never done it with a girl at school."

"Do you want to?"

"Sometimes," said the girl.

"It's always women? Older women?"

"It isn't as many as that sounds, Mrs. Lewis. And they usually want me before I want them."

"Did I want you?" said the woman. "Did you think I wanted you?"

"You didn't think it, but I knew you'd be willing," said the girl.

"You made me ask you to kiss me. That was pretty smart of you. Would you have if I didn't ask you?"

"Oh, but you wanted me to," said the girl.

"What do you do with boys, Marcy?"

"The same thing," said the girl.

"You've never had intercourse with a boy, or a man?"

"No. I might get pregnant."

"Do you dislike boys?"

"I like women better. Don't you?"

"Well, I did tonight, but I'm more used to men," said the woman. "What do you think of Lovey?"

"In this way, you mean?"

"In any way," said the woman.

"I think she wants a man to take the place of her father. She'll get married, but it won't be a boy. It'll be somebody older. She never talks about boys, only about older men. And her father."

"He had a lot of charm," said Dorothy.

"But you didn't love him. You had affairs with other men, didn't you?"

"Oh, we were both unfaithful, once in a while," said Dorothy.

"And you didn't care?" said Marcy.

"Of course I cared. You'll find out. Will you sleep better now?"

"Yes. Can I come here tomorrow night?"

"We have to be very careful, Marcy."

"Don't I know that!"

"How do you know so much at your age? Now you must get back to your room."

"I wish I could stay here all night. We were just right for each other, weren't we?"

"Yes, but we mustn't get excited again. Put on your nightgown and tiptoe back to your room."

"Think about me all day tomorrow and I'll think about

you," said the girl. She bent down and put a quick kiss on Dorothy's belly, got into her nightgown and left.

Now that she had made love to and been made love to by someone of her own sex, Dorothy immediately— and in momentary panic—questioned the element of wrongdoing in what she had done. All her life she had concurred in the belief that such actions were wrong, but as she lay in her bed in the darkened room she encouraged the doubts that were coming to her defense. *Why* was it wrong to do with a girl the very same things that she had done with a man? If it was not wrong with a man, why was it so terribly wrong with a girl? Why was *she* pleased that Lovey had not made love to Marcy or Marcy to her? What difference did it make? Who preached these beliefs? Well, a preacher preached them, and the preacher she knew best was a man who (her friends said) cautioned young boys not to masturbate— and then showed them how. The harshest and funniest things that were said about women who made love to women had been said by Billy Lewis, but in Berlin, in the final weeks of their long wedding trip, Billy had persuaded her to let a woman make love to her. What was funnier than a cow trying to mount another cow, but was it really so funny, a cow trying to mount another cow, a male dog trying to mount another male dog? It was in Nature, cow on cow, dog on dog, woman on woman. The girl had come to her room, and she was a lovely thing in her loneliness and emotional starvation, wanting a *woman* and wanting the woman to want her. It was in Nature and it was natural—and it was exciting, exciting, exciting, more exciting than a man doing the same thing. She lay there listening to the sounds of the house at night, wishing she could go to sleep and wake up the next night with the girl beside her. She absolved herself of wrongdoing, and soon fell asleep.

But when Ellen came in to bring her coffee and shut the windows Dorothy watched her carefully for any sign that that intuitive Irish intelligence was noticing anything unusual. *Yes.* "I notice you didn't open the windows," said Ellen. "Well, the night air's no good for you, I contend. The first time in a long while I come in this room that it wasn't cold as ice."

"I fell asleep reading this very dull legal paper," said Dorothy.

"Did you, now? And did you put the light out in your sleep?" To Ellen everyone in the world was a liar until proven innocent.

"I must have," said Dorothy.

"I'll be running your tub. Are you coming down for breakfast or having it here?"

"Is Miss Lovey awake?"

"No, ma'am. They're neither of them awake yet, but they want their breakfast at nine o'clock. In their rooms, in bed, with the fire going in both rooms, and the Philadelphia *Public Ledger* to be on Miss Bancroft's tray. That's the instructions Miss Lovey left. In unpacking Miss Bancroft I happened to take notice to something I think I ought to tell you."

"What was that?"

"I thought she looked a little old to be a friend of Miss Lovey's."

"Seventeen, I think," said Dorothy. "What did you see?"

"You know them things you insert in a certain place to guard against having a little one? You have one. You have a couple of them. They come in a cardboard box about so-big, made of rubber and with a tube of ointment."

"Called a vaginal diaphragm," said Dorothy.

"It couldn't be used for any other purpose, could it?" said Ellen.

"I shouldn't think so," said Dorothy.

"Well, she has one."

"That's rather surprising, but there could be an explanation for it," said Dorothy. "If she's engaged to be married, for instance, she may have been to see a doctor to get fitted for one."

"I don't know. I'm only telling you for what it's worth. She has one, and she's carrying it around with her."

"You don't miss anything, do you, Ellen?"

"Mighty little, ma'am," said Ellen. "It's our job to notice things. If I see a thing is wearing out, I ask you to get a new one. If I notice something is getting out of order, it's my job to report it to you. The other week I noticed the cord on the electric iron, and if I didn't report it to you the man said it could have started a fire. We don't want no fires in this house. It'd go up like tinder-wood."

"I fully understand, Ellen," said Dorothy. "Thank you."

"Thank you, ma'am," said Ellen. "And you'll be wanting your breakfast up here?"

"And the car at nine-thirty, tell Louis," said Dorothy. She picked up the legal paper and began to read it.

"One thing I don't have to worry about is a lot of legal papers, thanks be to God," said Ellen.

"Very fortunate," said Dorothy. In a small way, for the moment, she was fortunate to have legal business to attend to in the city. It enabled her to postpone for the time being her first encounter with Marcy; she was not yet ready for that, for the unpredictable look in those enormous brown eyes, for the unpredictable manner of shame or possessiveness. Would a girl who owned a pessary feel shame, or was she more likely to feel possessive? Dorothy was thankful that she could be out of the house before the girls finished their breakfast. She concentrated on the legal paper, and somehow in the morning light it began to make more sense to her. Clear thinking was easier in the morning—provided there had been no drinking after dinner the night before.

In the car Louis covered her knees with the robe, but she was in no mood to tease him with a glimpse of her thighs. "Mr. Williams's office on South Broad Street, and wait for me," she said.

"Yes, ma'am," said Louis. Celia Fuller had been the first to notice that Louis was a cowardly flirt, easily put in his place. Somewhere along the line he had undoubtedly gone to bed with the wife or daughter of an employer, but somewhere, too, he had been dismissed for getting fresh. At the moment Dorothy was immune to the twinkle in his eye, and it quickly faded. The day would come, she knew, when he would tuck the laprobe under her legs and test her susceptibility, but that day was not yet, and it was certainly not this day.

His voice came through the speaking-tube. "The young lady visiting Miss Lovey, ma'am?" he said.

"Miss Bancroft. Yes?"

"I seen her someplace before," said Louis.

"You may have. She goes to Hathaway. You must have seen her many times," said Dorothy.

"No, I'm in and out of there too quick in the mornings and the afternoons. It was somewheres else. Could she be from over around South Orange, that direction?"

"Her father is an army officer, stationed in Panama," said Dorothy.

"I guess that rules out South Orange, unless she was visiting somebody."

"You might ask *her*," said Dorothy.

"Yes, ma'am. I will," said Louis. "It would of been the year before last, when I was employed by Mr. R. W. Prescott, the toothpaste manufacturer. Two Cadillacs he had."

"Louis, I'm trying to concentrate on these papers."

"Excuse me, ma'am," said Louis.

Their journey took them past the Finnerton estate, which Dorothy had passed literally thousands of times and had visited on dozens of occasions. Usually she passed it without a second look, but today she found her attention inexplicably drawn to it. There was nothing new to see, and in any case the main house was partially hidden by great trees. *Anne Finnerton.* That was why she was looking in that direction. Anne Finnerton and her friend Claudia Greenley, whom Billy Lewis had nicknamed the Presidents because Anne strongly resembled Warren G. Harding and Claudia looked like Woodrow Wilson. It was one of Billy's more successful jokes. At the start of a hunt someone would always look around and ask, "Are the presidents here? We can't start without the presidents," and the presidents were nearly always there. "Riding sidesaddle, but fooling no one," Billy would say. Among the Lewis friends Anne and Claudia were a Lesbian institution, and Dorothy was suddenly grateful for them. For them, not to them. Whatever the future might hold for her the past contained a justifying precedent, an excuse for all unconventional conduct and all imaginable wrongdoing. Wrongdoing? Anne Finnerton and Claudia Greenley? There was piety in their devotion to each other and undeviating goodness in their work for the poor and the afflicted. What had she done that was so wrong, so wrong, so wrong? Something of her flesh had come up against some of Marcy's flesh and produced excitement and pleasure for them both. But what harm had been done, what cruelty or pain? Yes, the girl could be cruel, making her ask when she knew that Dorothy was ready to beg. But a man did that to a woman, and a woman did that to a man. "I am making too much of this," said Dorothy.

"What was that, ma'am?" said Louis.

"I didn't say anything."

"I thought you said we weren't making good time," said Louis.

"I didn't say anything at all, you're hearing things," said Dorothy.

"Yes, ma'am," said Louis. "Forever hearing things."

At Grafton Williams's office Joe Fuller was also waiting.

"I don't need to ask after one look at you two," said Dorothy.

"Evans said you were asking too much. Or *we're* asking too much, to put it that way," said Grafton Williams.

"In any case, we're going to have to find another buyer," said Joe Fuller.

"Did you read that thing I gave you to read?" said Grafton.

"I plowed through it. It's a petition, I know that. Such

a strange word to be using in the Twentieth Century. Petitioning a judge that would give his right arm if I let him in our kitchen door."

"Nevertheless a judge," said Grafton. "I asume you'll sign this petition. I'll need your signature on five copies. Now to get back to the Willingham Road parcel. I've had what may be a piece of good news this morning, although you may not consider it good. A lawyer friend of mine, a Catholic, has a client who's in a mood to found a Catholic Groton. He has the money. But there are certain conditions. The school has to be near Philadelphia, and it has to be named after his father. Oh, there are other conditions as well, and the only one that really interests us is the nearness to Philadelphia. My lawyer friend believes that your house would be just about perfect, if you didn't ask too much. But he'd want the whole property, including the Willingham Road parcel. In other words, the wall and everything behind it. Now here's the fly in the ointment. Assuming for the moment that you'd be willing to sell the whole property, we'd have to take the Willingham Road parcel off the market. The question is, are you so attached to the house and grounds that you want to go on living there, or would you sell? The alternative is, we sell bits and pieces so that you can afford to go on living there. Because that's the way it's going to be, Dorothy, and Joe agrees with me. You and Lovey can be very well off, provided your income isn't eaten up by taxes and the expenses of keeping up that size property. Billy was a fine horseman, but when it came to financial matters, he was—impetuous, let us say. In two years, he lost over $600,000. In fifteen years—well, he had just the opposite of the magic touch."

"God knows *I* tried to tell him often enough," said Joe Fuller.

"Oh, I know you did, Joe," said Dorothy.

"No, there were times you never knew about," said Joe.

"I suppose so," said Dorothy. "Well, I guessed that things weren't so good, and this is what you'd call breaking it to me gently."

"There's no cause for alarm, mind you," said Grafton Williams. "You have your own money, and Lovey has a little. But Cardiff House is a thing of the past."

"Cardiff House! Billy stopped calling it that when his father died," said Dorothy.

"Yes, and that long ago it was a thing of the past," said Grafton.

"All of the old man's houses were named after places in Wales," said Joe Fuller.

"He could have had a genuine castle for what he spent

on them—if the castle had been in Wales. But not this country."

"I'll do whatever you say, Grafton. You and Joe. I do wish I could keep the house till Lovey comes out. A year from now she'll be eighteen. Can I do that?"

"That'd be a very expensive coming-out party," said Grafton.

"I'd give her the party," said Joe Fuller. "I'd like to anyway. But Dorothy, you mustn't stand in the way of a possible sale. Celia and I would be delighted to have her come out at our house, and after all it was my horse that—"

"Oh, Joe, not that again. You haven't mentioned that horse in ages."

"And Billy never did either. But he must have thought at least once a day that it was my horse. And you don't blame the horse in a case like that, you blame the owner."

"Not if you have any sense, you don't," said Dorothy.

"Of course not," said Grafton.

Joe Fuller laughed a private laugh. "There we were, I was his best friend, he was my best friend, all our lives, in spite of the fact that we had reason to hate each other. My horse cost him the sight of one eye, and he screwed Celia before I did."

"Now just a minute, there, Joe," said Grafton Williams. "I don't like that kind of talk, and in my office I'm not going to have it."

"Why not? It's no news to Dorothy, and I'll bet it's no news to you."

"That's not the point," said Grafton.

"Oh, bullshit, Grafton," said Joe Fuller.

"Now look here, Joe. In this office you have to behave yourself. You're not in a stable here, and I won't have you talking as if you were. I don't like it one bit. Now you apologize to Dorothy."

"Dorothy, I'm sorry I said Billy screwed Celia before I did, and I'm sorry I said bullshit. And if you weren't present, I'd tell Grafton to go fuck himself."

"That's enough for today," said Grafton. "The nasty little boy can leave this instant."

"Thank you, counselor. I could do with a drink along about now," said Joe Fuller. He got his hat and coat off the clothes-tree and departed.

"You never know," said Grafton. "Last night he was certainly sober when he left our house. He had one cocktail, wine with dinner, a brandy, and then not more than three drinks after dinner. It came to about one drink an hour. Didn't you think he was sober?"

"He was, when I last saw him. But we don't know what he did after he got home," said Dorothy. "Sometimes he sits there all night, playing the Victrola, listening to the radio."

"He does?"

"He may not even have gone to bed," said Dorothy.

"He smelled rather strongly of hair tonic when he came in."

"Then I'm sure he hadn't been to bed," said Dorothy. "The butler brings him his coffee and shaves him, and he takes a shower and gets dressed. I know that, because he's been doing it for years. Billy told me that Joe never goes to bed the night before he's going to hunt."

"That could turn out to be a very dangerous habit," said Grafton.

"If he didn't drink the night before, he'd never hunt," said Dorothy.

"Oh, I see," said Grafton. "I know lawyers that have to get drunk the night before they're going into court."

"Exactly," said Dorothy. "Now he'll go to the club and have some more to drink, and lunch, and the chauffeur will come and get him and take him home."

"I've never seen him drunk at lunch. But of course I don't go to the club every day. I usually have a sandwich and a glass of milk here. I get some of my best work done between half-past twelve and two o'clock. No telephone interrupting me. Well, I'm sorry to learn this about Joe. He's ten years younger than I, so we've never been very close, and our interests are different, to say the least. I don't know the first thing about horses and never did. Cousin Claudia Greenley is the only member of my generation to go in for riding, but of course the family always said she should have been a boy."

"You don't think you should have been a girl, do you, Grafton?" said Dorothy.

"Good Lord, no. Although now that you mention it, I have my gardening, and my tennis, neither of which interests Claudia. I couldn't imagine what it would be like to be a woman." He put his hand to his upper lip and touched his moustache. "At least I wouldn't have to shave every day. Well, Dorothy, I'll have another talk with my Catholic friend, and then discuss the outcome of my conversation with Joe, if he's in a fit condition. Your own affairs, by the way, are in good shape. At least Billy never tampered with them. You have between twelve and fourteen thousand a year you can count on."

"Is that all?" said Dorothy.

"My dear Dorothy, when Billy's estate is finally

settled, your twelve thousand a year will represent about one third of your total income. I thought you understood that the last time you were here."

"I guess I didn't follow you," said Dorothy. "Thirty-six thousand a year. That isn't much, is it?"

"Most people would think it was a lot. But you couldn't live on the income of your income as some of our friends do. You can't even live on your present scale on thirty-six thousand a year. Let me prepare you a schedule of your present expenses versus income, with my suggestions on where you can economize. Will you read it, and follow it, if I do?"

"I don't seem to have much choice, do I?" said Dorothy.

"Not really, no," said Grafton. "You can go into debt, but that wouldn't be fair to yourself or to Lovey."

"You're beginning to put the fear of God into me, Grafton," said Dorothy.

"The fear of God and the fear of debt keep people out of trouble," he said.

"I wonder," said Dorothy.

"Well, let's put it this way," said Grafton. "The fear of debt puts the fear of God into some people. I know that there'd be more divorces if people could afford them. I don't touch divorce cases, but I can't help but learn what it is that keeps some marriages intact, right here in Philadelphia. I'd be the last to claim that all my clients live in perfect connubial bliss."

"Did you know about Celia and Billy? I can't help asking you that," said Dorothy.

He hesitated before answering. "I wish you hadn't asked me. But since you did, I'll admit that as Joe said, it wasn't news to me."

"It wasn't news to anybody," said Dorothy.

"It's a strange thing about Philadelphia, Dorothy. Whenever I hear a piece of gossip, old or new, I always seem to have heard it before. When I was in college, for instance, I heard a scandalous story about an uncle of mine. Uncle George Greenley, as a matter of fact."

"That he had a mistress, an opera singer," said Dorothy.

"That's the story. Famous Philadelphia scandals. Well, when I heard the story I wasn't shocked or surprised, because it seemed to me that I'd known it for years. But when I checked back on it, I couldn't have known it for years, because this clandestine relationship had only been in existence a few months, dating from the opera singer's arrival in Philadelphia. Uncle George hadn't even met the questionable lady in question more than a few months before I got the report. I suppose the reason I wasn't surprised was that I had always taken for granted that Uncle George was the sort of man who would have a mistress an opera singer. And that's the interesting thing about Philadelphia. We all know each other so well that mere facts only confirm what we've always known."

"Well, that's a frightening thing, too," said Dorothy.

"Yes, in some cases. But it's also reassuring to know that if a lie is told about you, most people will know it's a lie. Dorothy, there weren't many people my age who didn't believe the rumor that Joe Fuller repeated this morning. We all knew both parties, and the rumor wasn't uh—anomalous."

"In language that I can understand, it was like Billy to sleep with Celia and like Celia to sleep with Billy," said Dorothy.

"I believe that sleeping together was only a turn of phrase. As I recall, the assignations took place in a hay loft and the lovers were discovered by a servant's child looking for hen's eggs."

"That's true. That's the way Billy told it to me. The whole thing was ridiculously funny."

"Very sporting of you to say, but the young lady's

father didn't think it was so funny at the time and neither did her brother. And Joe doesn't think so now. Therefore it isn't so funny, Dorothy. Let me be very serious and old-fashioned for a moment. May I?"

"Of course," said Dorothy.

"I as your lawyer know your true age. Thirty-eight. I'm fifty-two, and more the product of the Victorian era than you are, although you were born in it. But you mustn't go too much against the influences and conditions that affected the first years of your childhood and young girlhood. Today we have bobbed hair and short skirts and bootleg gin, and our standards are changing by the minute, it seems to me. But are they really? You pretend not to care that your husband and your best friend had an affair before you were married. But don't you? Joe cares, always has and always will. The bitterness is there, very close to the surface. It only took a reminder of his guilt about Billy's blindness to stir up the bitterness, and with unpleasant consequences. He has absolutely no right to talk that way when I'm present, no matter how you let him talk at other times. I'm a man, and I'm not shocked by naughty words, but I am shocked by Joe's deliberate disrespect to you *in front of me*. I was ready to put him out of my office by force, if necessary. And when we've finished with the business of Billy's estate, Joe Fuller will never again be welcome in this office. He has no dignity of his own, no respect for others. He is *not* a gentleman. He is a boor, whatever made him that way."

"Too much to drink," said Dorothy.

"No excuse. We have a clerk in this office who's dying of an incurable, painful disease, but he behaves like a gentleman even if his father happens to have been a streetcar conductor. What I'm getting at, Dorothy, is that I want to warn you that Joe Fuller is not quite the friend that you believe him to be, that Billy believed him to be, and that I believed him to be. That he may even have believed himself to be. I never found him very attractive. Spoiled. Too pleased with himself. But with the difference in our ages, I never had to see him much. Also, I was undoubtedly prejudiced by the fact that his grandfather and my grandfather had a falling-out over a business matter, with the result that my grandfather lost everything and his grandfather became a millionaire. Consequently, we didn't genuflect every time we heard the name Fuller. My father and Joe's father were polite to each other, but hardly more than that. Then when Billy was making his will I tried to suggest that someone with a better knowledge of business be made executor.

Billy wouldn't hear of it. Joe was a very clever business man. Didn't go to an office every day, but a very clever business man. Hmm. Well, I will agree now that Joe Fuller made money for Joe Fuller. But by Jove he never made any for Billy Lewis. As far as I've been able to determine, the biggest losses Billy incurred were in stocks that Joe made a killing in. Now that could be explained if it only happened once or twice, but I've discovered that it happened repeatedly. Billy would buy a stock, the price would fall, and Joe would take it off his hands, as they say. Then the stock would double and sometimes triple in price, and Joe would make his killing. The only consolation Billy had was that if he had held on to the stock, he would have made a pile of money. But it's very strange indeed that his best friend was always ready to buy the stock cheap and never once, apparently, made him hold on to it a little longer. Dorothy, I'm convinced, without an ounce of proof, that Joe Fuller deliberately broke Billy. I could go to prison for such a statement. But before I do, I might make Joe Fuller very uncomfortable and possibly take him to prison with me. The deeper I get into this thing, the more I believe that I may come upon something that will confirm my suspicions of Joe Fuller. If I do, though, it'll only be luck. Naturally there are no letters to back me up. A man buys stock, the stock goes down, he sells it to his best friend. I'd have a heck of a hard time proving any wrongdoing there."

"Any what?"

"Any wrongdoing. But if I'm ever sure enough of my ground, I might be able to convince Joe that the ethical thing would be to make some contribution to Billy's estate. Here we get into legal technicalities, but a lawyer can always find a way to accept money for a client. In this case, you and Lovey. Extra-legally, I'm convinced that Joe Fuller owes you a million dollars. Legally, he doesn't owe you a darn cent. Indeed, he could argue that if he hadn't bought Billy's stock, Billy's losses would have been greater."

"I don't want you to do anything about Joe," said Dorothy.

"There isn't much chance that I can. But are you saying that you don't want me to try?"

"I'm saying that I don't want you to embarrass him in any way," said Dorothy.

"Why on earth not, Dorothy? In my own mind I'm convinced that he rooked you out of a million dollars."

"He didn't rook me out of anything, and you say yourself that you can't prove any wrongdoing. So I want you to give him the benefit of the doubt."

"Why?" said Grafton Williams.

"Well, Grafton, you know us all so well. Why don't you take a guess?"

He looked at her, and looked away. He stroked his moustache with his forefinger, first the right side and then the left. Then the right side with his thumb and the left side with his forefinger. He finished this unconscious bit of grooming and placed his fingers on the desk. "Very well," he said. "I've taken my guess."

"And are you surprised?" said Dorothy.

"No, but you might be," said Grafton.

"Might I?" she said.

"Yes, you might, and that's all I'm going to say about it," he said.

"Why, Grafton, you're turning coy on me," she said.

"Call it that if you wish," he said.

She had a new respect for him. It would have been so easy for a man like Grafton Williams—*for Grafton Williams*—to accept her implication without questioning it. But he questioned it, and the very fact of his questioning it raised her opinion of him and his mind, his instincts, his humanity. Four times in her married life she had had sexual intercourse of one kind or another with Joe Fuller: once in his bed, when he had a broken ankle; once on the ground, behind the tennis court; and twice in his car when he opened his trousers and asked her to kiss him. To that extent she had had an affair with Joe Fuller. But Grafton Williams had refused to accept her implication of a relationship that was more than casual erotic encounters. The man was more astute than she had ever realized, even though he was technically in error. It now seemed possible that this unprepossessing man, with his bow tie and grey worsted suit and his Phi Beta Kappa key swinging against his chest, was more worldly than anyone knew. At another time, in other circumstances, she might be able to trust him fully. But not now. It was on impulse, but a strong impulse, that she had insisted on protecting Joe Fuller from embarrassment. The girl Marcy was turning out to be something besides a cautious sensualist. Indeed, she could do with more caution. To leave a pessary where a chambermaid would discover it was a poor example of her discretion, and the pessary was evidence that she was a liar. A man, or men were in her life, and Dorothy chose to believe it was men. The girl had easily and completely seduced her, so easily and so completely that it bespoke a superior and special intelligence, and of that intelligence and the related sensuality Dorothy was afraid. In her fear she could think of only one person as a dependable ally, and that was Joe Fuller. In spite of all his shortcomings, and a little because of them, he was the human being she would go to for help if help were needed. One turned to a bounder more readily than to a priest, hoping that the bounder would let one off with a lighter penance. Dorothy could imgaine the heavy humor of Joe Fuller if she had to confess to him. "Say, I'd like to be there with you two," he would say. But if anything had to be done to keep Marcy quiet, Joe Fuller was the friend to do it. The friend. "As a friend, Dorothy, just as a friend," he had said to her those times in the car. And as a friend she had obliged him. It was hilariously ironic now to learn that he was also costing her a million dollars, and avenging himself for Billy and Celia.

"Well, I must go," said Dorothy. "I'm having a skating party for Lovey. She has a house guest, a perfectly adorable girl. Father's in the army in Panama, and Lovey just couldn't stand to see her cooped up at Hathaway. When I say she's adorable, I don't really know her, but I'm sure the boys will like her."

"If she's half as nice as Lovey," said Grafton. "That's a real kid. You have to hand it to a young girl that has the spunk to just get up and leave a place like Miss Brandon's. The women around Philadelphia that wish they'd had as much spunk! I'll see you to the elevator."

"Enjoy your milk and sandwich, Grafton," said Dorothy.

"Would you—could I offer you—"

"No, I'd be much worse than the telephone. But thanks," she said.

"Dorothy, we'll pull out of this without undue discomfort. It won't even be genteel poverty. A smaller place, fewer servants. Oh, and by the way, if Guy Glynn ever wants to come and work for me, I'd be glad to have him. Naturally I'd never offer him a job while—ah, here we are. Down! Going down, please."

As she was driving through the park the beauties of the snow-dressed trees and the glistening frozen river were lost on Dorothy. The park was semi-country; real country minutes away, and minutes away was the face, the eyes of the girl and whatever they would tell her in that first look. "Please be nice to me," said Dorothy. "I won't do anything bad to you."

Already the cars with chauffeurs were lining up to unload the guests. "Goodness, what time is it?" said Dorothy.

"I have five minutes of two, ma'am," said Louis. "It took us longer today. Do you want me to take you around to the kitchen door?"

"A very good idea, Louis," said Dorothy.

They swung off at the fork that led to the back of the house, garage, and stables. Dorothy entered the kitchen and passed through to the front hall.

"Mummy, where *were* you? I thought you'd never get here,"

"Very sorry. There's still a lot of snow on the roads,

you know. And besides, it's your party, Lovey. You're really the hostess, not I."

"I know, but we've had a crisis," said Lovey. "Guy says it isn't safe to skate on the pond. The ice isn't thick enough."

"Well, if Guy says so, he knows," said Dorothy. "But there are other places in the neighborhood."

"I know there are, and that's where we're going. Max Fuller said their tennis court is flooded and the ice is all right there."

"Have you asked Mrs. Fuller?"

"Max is calling her now," said Lovey. "Here he is. What's the answer, Max?"

"All settled," said Max Fuller. He was a husky boy in a thick white sweater turned inside out, riding breeches and golf stockings, and chauffeur's gauntlets tucked under his arm. "How do you do, Aunt Dorothy."

"Apparently you've saved the day," said Dorothy. "All right, Lovey, take your friends over to the Fullers' and then come back here for tea. By the way, where's your house guest?"

"She's around somewhere. There she is, talking to Warty Zabriskie." Marcy, in skating tights and a short skirted jacket, was engaged in conversation with Wharton Zabriskie, a tall thin boy who was already known as a

snake and a tea-fighter as well as being heir presumptive
to his mother's considerable share of the Pennsylvania
Railroad. "*Yes*, Mummy, she's wearing your skating outfit
but I told her she could."

"Looks better on her," said Dorothy.

"That's how we spent the morning. Inspecting your
wardrobe," said Lovey.

"All right, get along with you," said Dorothy.

Lovey announced the slight change in plans, and the
guests made for the front door. Some of the better-
mannered came and spoke to Dorothy on their way out,
and Marcy hung back to be the last. She took the hem
of her skirt in her fingertips and expanded it like a
dancer.

"Did Lovey tell you?" said the girl.

"Yes, it looks very well on you."

The girl leaned forward and spoke softly. "I love it
because it's yours."

"Oh, Marcy—thank you," said Dorothy.

"I'll see you *later?*" said the girl.

"Yes, dear," said Dorothy.

The humiliating thing was to be fully aware of the
girl's insincerity and yet to be so grateful for the show
of tenderness. Dorothy was used to the compliments of
men, the perfunctorily polite compliments and the more

meaningful overtures, but the girl was not so much being nice to her as enjoying her own strength. Did Lovey say that Marcy had been trying on Dorothy's dresses that morning? No, she had not said that, but Dorothy wished it were true. Did Marcy speak the truth when she said she loved the skating outfit because it was Dorothy's? No, but Dorothy wanted to believe her and was titillated by the sight of her in it. What instinct had so quickly drawn the girl to the Zabriskie boy, who already had the beginnings of an unsavory reputation among his contemporaries and their mothers? Ah, but the girl would be able to handle him, and Dorothy was strangely proud of her for that.

It was dark when the young came back from skating and trooped in for hot chocolate and tea. Dorothy stayed out of sight; it was Lovey's party, and apparently a success. "Mum, we've all been asked to Mrs. Zabriskie's. Is it all right if we go?" said Lovey.

"Asked by Mrs. Zabriskie or by Warty?" said Dorothy.

"By him, first, but he called up. It's pot luck, come as we are, and so forth."

"Chaperoned by Mrs. Zabriskie?" said Dorothy.

"Well, no. But by a houseful of butlers and maids. All the others are going that can, that haven't got something else to do. Warty has a whole lot of new records, and it's going to be great. Warty is really smitten by Marcy."

"How late will it last?"

"Oh—midnight?"

"All right, but no later," said Dorothy.

It was closer to two o'clock when Lovey and Marcy got home, and past three when the girl opened the door of Dorothy's room and whispered. "Are you awake?"

"Yes, come in," said Dorothy. She switched on her reading lamp, and the girl got directly into bed with her, put her arms around her and kissed her on the mouth. "Did you miss me?" said the girl. "Are you cross with me?"

"I can't be cross with you, and I'm afraid you know it," said Dorothy.

"Don't you want me to know it?" said the girl. "We don't have to pretend to one another, do we?"

"No, and that's what I've been thinking, Marcy."

"You're sorry. You'd like me to leave, and never come back."

"If you can guess that much, you can guess why," said Dorothy.

"Of course I can guess why," said the girl. "You're ashamed."

"Yes, I am," said Dorothy.

"But you're not a girl at Hathaway. You can do whatever you want to do. You're rich and prominent and all that. You don't have to care."

"You're forgetting Lovey," said Dorothy.

"No I'm not. I like Lovey. She's been nicer to me than anyone else at school. But she's not a baby. She ran away from one school and got into Hathaway without any trouble at all. Because you're rich and prominent. If her mother gets into trouble they're not going to blame her— and what if they do? But *she's* not going to get into trouble, and neither are you. The only one that can really get into trouble is me." The girl put her hand on Dorothy's breast and squeezed gently. "I thought of you all day. You thrill me. Wearing your tights thrilled me. But not as much as you can when I'm here with you. Isn't it nice that I can thrill you too?"

"It's nice, but you know it's wrong," said Dorothy.

"You can make it wrong by thinking it's wrong, but I don't think it *is* wrong. Otherwise why do we feel this way? If you think it's wrong don't you kiss me, but I'll kiss you, because I like to."

"I like to kiss you," said the woman.

"I know you do," said the girl. "Let's kiss each other at the same time. Have you ever done that?"

"With a man," said Dorothy.

"Will you try it with me?" said Marcy.

"Yes," said Dorothy.

Then after a while the girl lay beside her and kissed the palm of her hand and her fingertips. "Tomorrow's my last night," said the girl.

"Tomorrow is?" said the woman.

"I'm leaving the next afternoon. That'll be four days and three nights," said the girl. "Then I won't see you again, maybe ever. What if I never see you again? Will you be sad?"

"Of course I will. But I am going to see you again. When is your spring vacation?"

"Easter, a long way off."

"But don't you get weekends sometimes?"

"I don't, because my family didn't say I could. They have to give permission ahead of time."

"If I wrote to them and wrote to Miss Roberts?" said Dorothy.

"Wait a while. When you want me again, you can tell old Ida Van Fleet Roberts. I think she'd like me instead of Miss King, but she's afraid to try. I wonder if she and Miss King ever do what we just did? I'd rather do it with Miss King than with Miss Roberts, wouldn't you?"

"I can't imagine doing it with anyone but you."

"Or a man," said the girl.

"Have you done that with a man, Marcy?"

"Not what we did. I've done the other, the usual thing."

"I was pretty sure of that," said Dorothy.

"But I don't like anything with a man, or a boy, or a member of the male sex. I don't like men or boys or young girls or skinny flat-chested women. You're just right. Mrs. Zabriskie is almost right. I met her tonight. They got home just before we left. But her bust isn't as nice as yours. Nothing to it. I guess I like women that are built like me, and older. I get notes from girls at school. It's fun trying to guess who they're from. I'm pretty sure that one was from the richest girl in school. Her father owns a steamship line, and if I were sure it was she, then I wouldn't have to depend on army transportation. Wouldn't it be nice to have a pass to go anywhere without paying?"

"The Zabriskies have a railroad pass, good on any railroad in the United States," said Dorothy.

"Why do they call him Warty? He doesn't have warts."

"Short for Wharton. W, h, a, r, t, o, n. His mother was Zella Wharton."

"He was feeling me up all evening. I think your tights got him all excited."

"He's going to Princeton next year, Marcy."

"So he told me."

"Remember last night, you were talking about a Princeton millionaire?"

"Yes I was, wasn't I? Maybe if you'll lend me your tights again sometime that'll solve all my problems."

"I'm going to give you the skating costume. I've given up skating, and they fit you so well," said Dorothy.

"If I married him I wouldn't be living very far from you. You could come and see me any time you wanted to. We could take baths together and spend whole nights together. When will he be twenty-one, do you know?"

"Yes, he's nineteen now," said Dorothy.

"I wish I could stay here all night, cuddled up with you. I get terribly exciting dreams, and it'd be nice to wake up and sort of make the dreams come true. Who do you dream about? Men?"

"Sometimes."

"I do sometimes, but my most exciting dreams are about women. I'll bet I dream about you when I go back to school."

"Speaking of dreams, Marcy?"

"I know, and I hate to leave this nice warm bed and you." She got out of bed and stood naked with her arms outstretched their full length. "Dream about me," she said. "Dream something very wicked, and think about it all day tomorrow." She blew a kiss to Dorothy and left.

Alone, Dorothy lit a cigarette and lay back on her pillow and wondered why she felt neither guilt nor fear, but rather a glow of physical well-being and spiritual regeneration. She soon found the answer. The girl, relaxed after the intense physical pleasure, had revealed her mentality as freely as though her venality were an attribute in which to take pride, like her body. She was still potentially troublesome, but she wanted so many things that she was less of a threat than if she had wanted only one major thing. She could be placated with an old skating costume, while being denied something like free access to the house; pennies instead of dollars. It was so early in her infatuation with the girl that Dorothy was still atingle with the excitement of the taboo, but already the element of fear had been reduced by the girl's inadvertent admission that she could be had cheaply. With this discovery Dorothy committed herself to the pleasurable contemplation of an affair without fear. She could even concede some thanks to the girl for showing her that all her life she had been having intermittent accesses of desire for members of her own sex. The incident in Berlin on her wedding trip had had the effect of postponing and frustrating the next experiment; the German woman had been more interested in pleasing Billy than her, and Billy had confused her by submitting her to the German woman's intimacies. "You didn't like that," Billy had said.

"No, but I'll do whatever you like," said Dorothy.

"Well, we'll never do that again," said Billy (and he had kept his word).

"But why did you like it?" said Dorothy.

"I don't know," said Billy.

"If I *had* liked it you might have been sorry," said Dorothy.

"Yes, I would have been jealous," said Billy. "But don't worry, we'll never do it again." He not only kept his word but he never in any way referred to the incident, and for him at least it seemed to have been obliterated from their connubial experience. Nearly so it was with Dorothy as well, but with the difference that whenever she was attracted by another girl her total recall of the Berlin incident would remind her of what her yielding to the attraction would lead to. Among her women friends she became known as the least demonstrative girl of them all. "You

could be gone a whole year and Dorothy wouldn't even
shake hands with you when you got home," Celia Fuller
once said. But Dorothy's inhibition was not complete. If
she was attracted by a newcomer or by an old friend in
an especially beautiful dress, she would make herself de-
sirable to Billy, and she knew how. Her vulnerability to
the sharp-eyed Marcy Bancroft was increased by the long
period of continence between Billy's fatal accident and
Marcy's first appearance. A couple of times during that
period she had caught Joe Fuller studying her, and she
had caught herself studying Joe Fuller. What she had
done for him "as a friend" he might as a friend do for her.
But now she did not need Joe Fuller; there was Marcy.

The third night with Marcy was curiously like the
night with the German woman in Berlin, as though
Dorothy instead of Billy had hired a professional, and
Marcy was making the effort to please the one who had
hired her. "Did you dream about me, like I told you to?"
said Marcy. "Something very wicked?"

"Of course not," said Dorothy. "You can't just dream
because you want to."

"I know some things," said the girl. "To do," she
added. "You could hurt me."

"I wouldn't hurt you for the world," said Dorothy.

"Maybe I'd like it. Or maybe you'd like me to hurt you."

"I don't like to be hurt."

"I don't mean seriously hurt. Have you got a needle?"

"I won't do that, Marcy, and I won't let you do it to me."

"Oh, you've heard about that?"

"Of course, and worse things than that. But you mustn't do them."

"If I like to I will," said the girl. "I'll let you scratch me with a safety razor."

"No, no," said the woman. "Marcy, you shock me, you really do."

"I know I do. I want to."

"Why?"

"Because you're so innocent. I know girls that like to do things to children, but I don't. I'm just the opposite. Do you know what a man told me? He told me I was the most corrupt girl he ever knew."

"And that pleased you, obviously," said the woman.

"I didn't like 'corrupt' but I liked shocking him. They all think I'm a dumb little innocent. But I'm not. He gave me fifty dollars not to tell anybody what *he* liked to do."

"Poor man," said the woman.

"Poor man, nothing. He could do the same thing with his wife, but she wouldn't let him. So he does it with the daughter of his best friend."

"Your godfather, I suppose."

"Yes, but I won't tell you what he does. If it ever got out he'd have to resign his commission. Not that you'd ever tell anybody, but I'm an army brat and you're a civilian."

"If he were a civilian, would you be so loyal?"

"I'm not going to tell anybody about us, if that's what you mean. I have a crush on you. Worse than that, I guess. I have a passion for you. I don't often get passions for people."

"Is that the same as love, Marcy?"

"Love? I love my parents, and that's all. Besides, you don't love me. You love Lovey. You didn't even love Mr. Lewis."

"How do you know that?"

"I asked Lovey, and she didn't think you did."

"Well, she was wrong."

"Oh, you have to say that, but you didn't. I can tell. I can always tell."

"This time you're wrong, Marcy. I did love Mr. Lewis."

"You like to think so because he was your husband and he was killed, but you didn't. Him or any other man. You're not a man's woman. I can tell, I can always tell. I'm not a man's woman either, don't forget that. If I marry Warty Zabriskie, it won't be because I love him."

"Oh, are you going to marry Warty?"

"I could if I saw him often enough," said the girl.

"You don't know Mrs. Zabriskie."

"I know her better than she knows me, and I know her son better than she knows him. You know what the southern girls say. He's all hot and bothered, and I'm going to keep him that way. Last night, his hand under my skirt, and got nowhere. Tonight, no hand up my skirt but accidentally on my teats on the outside. Tomorrow he wants to drive me back to school in their car. Maybe I'll let him soul-kiss me just once, but that's all. The funny thing is, I don't really dislike him. If we were rich and he was poor, I'd show him a good time. He's so horny."

"Would you rather marry him than finish Vassar? With all that your parents have given up for your education?"

"If he were twenty-one I'd marry him tomorrow."

"All right, I'll do what I can to help you," said Dorothy. "As much for his sake as for yours."

"Why do you say that?" said the girl.

"Because I think you'd be good for him. He's rather like my husband when he was that age."

"And I'm like you?" said the girl.

"To some extent, in some ways. Anyhow, you could have a good marriage, as good as most. But if I were you, Marcy, I'd stop giving pleasure to older men and things like that. I know Mrs. Zabriskie very well, and she's going to find out everything she can about you."

"Tell her you and I are queer for each other, and all the rest is a pack of lies."

"Is that what we are? Queer for each other?" said the woman.

"You really don't know anything, do you?" said the girl.

"I never heard that expression," said the woman.

Some days, when Dorothy had reason to be in Philadelphia in the morning, she would drop Lovey at school. "You seem to be going in much oftener," said Lovey, a few weeks after the Christmas holidays.

"I am, and I will be," said Dorothy. "Your father's estate is much more complicated than we thought."

"Shall I start worrying about it?" said Lovey.

"No. But there's a possibility that we may have to sell the house. Some Catholics want to buy it for a school, and if they offer us enough money, we'll sell. The upkeep is just too much for us. We can talk about it when you have more time."

"We can talk about it now, Mummy"

"Very sketchily, but I don't want to keep you in the dark any more than I have to," said Dorothy.

"Don't keep me in the dark at all," said Lovey. "If we're going to have to sell, we're going to have to sell."

"Well, I have a good income of my own, irrespective of your father's estate. But my income isn't big enough to go on living in a big house with a lot of fixed expenses and taxes. It's just pouring the money down the drain. On the other hand, if I reduce our expenses we can live very comfortably. I was rather hoping we could live there till you got married, but we can't. If I kept the house two more years, I'd have to begin spending capital, and that's dangerous. And unnecessary. I'd have to dip into capital so that the house and grounds wouldn't begin to show neglect. And if it showed neglect, the value would go down fast. Do you understand this so far?"

"Yes, I can see how that would be. Now let me say something?"

"Of course."

"I loved the house and the whole place and having servants and so on. But it was never our house. It was Grandpa Lewis's house. It wasn't even Daddy's house as much as Grandpa's. Daddy had his one room, his den, that he had full of his own things. But he spent more time out in the stable than in the house. And it was never your house either. It was home, where we lived, but most of the furniture and stuff was in the house when you married Daddy, wasn't it?"

"Practically all of it except our wedding presents," said Dorothy.

"Well, that's really all I have to say, I guess," said Lovey.

"Were you unhappy living there?"

"No, not exactly. But when I grew up I began to wonder. Why was I like Daddy, spending as much time as I could with Guy in his garden, and out at the stable and every place but inside? Maybe it would have been different if it'd been yours and Daddy's house from the beginning, and not Grandpa's. It isn't even a terribly old house. It's not old, it's not new, it's just big. And when I get married I'll never live there. I'd rather live in Manayunk, in my own house."

"All right. That settles it. Mr. Williams will be very glad to hear that. And Uncle Joe.Fuller. By the way, the Fullers want to give you your coming-out party, at their house."

"Then just tell them that I'm not coming out."

"But you have to come out, Lovey. Not only for yourself but for your own daughters."

"You forget, I haven't got any daughters," said Lovey.

"Every girl that ever came out probably fought it in the beginning, but they're all glad they did. I was the same way, and your daughter will be the same and her daughter and her daughter. Your father wanted you to come out as much as I did."

"Then why didn't he make enough money so we could afford it, instead of taking charity from the Fullers?"

"That's not fair, and not very nice. And not true. We can afford a party, I can afford a party for you. But Mr. and Mrs. Fuller would like to have it at their house."

"Mr. and Mrs. Joseph Fuller . . . small dance . . . to meet the daughter of Mr. and Mrs. F. Willingham Lewis," said Lovey. "*No.*"

"Well, we've settled enough for one morning without going into that," said Dorothy.

"That's settled too, Mummy. If the Fullers want to have a party, they can. But I'm not going to be the excuse for it, and that's final. And don't say, 'We'll see.' "

The car stopped, Lovey gave her mother a light buss on the cheek and got out. "Mr. Williams's office, Louis," said Dorothy. Against her will she looked among the classroom-bound girls for Marcy Bancroft, but she was not to be seen.

At that moment, in fact, Marcy Bancroft was waiting

in Ida Van Fleet Roberts's outer office. It was very important if Ida Roberts would send for her to appear immediately after morning assembly, making the girl late for the day's first class. Presently Ida entered the anteroom, gripping her Bible with its colored ribbons and a sheet of typewritten announcements. She nodded and muttered good-morning to Marcy, the typist, and a salesman who had an over-filled brief case on his lap. She stopped and spoke to the salesman. "I'm sorry, I won't be able to see you this morning, Mr. Snodgrass. Come back late this afternoon. Marcy, will you come in, please?"

"Yes, Miss Roberts," said the girl.

Ida Roberts steadied herself behind her desk. "Sit down, Marcy," she said, and stared at the girl. "Have you any idea why I sent for you?"

"No, but it must be serious," said the girl.

"Think a moment," said Ida Roberts.

"Something's happened to my family?" said the girl. "A cablegram?"

"Think again."

"I haven't the faintest idea, honestly I haven't," said the girl.

Ida Roberts opened the desk drawer with a key. "I have something of yours here. You had it hidden very carefully, but it was discovered during breakfast. Now of course you know what it is."

"I'm not sure," said the girl.

"Oh, you have more than one contraband article in your possession? Well, after seeing this I don't doubt that for a minute."

"What is it?"

"I'm not even going to open the box. You'll recognize the box. Now you know what it is?"

"Yes."

"You realize that this means instant expulsion."

"Why?"

"*Why?* In all my years as teacher and headmistress of this school, no girl has ever been caught with an apparatus like this. Where did you get it?"

"From my godmother."

"Your godmother? The woman at West Point? She gave it to you?"

"No, I took it from her. I found it in her bathroom."

"I don't believe you," said Ida Roberts. "How did you know what it was?"

"It says on the box," said the girl.

"In very circumspect language."

"But what else could it be?"

"I won't have you matching wits with me, young lady. Have you ever used this thing?"

"No," said the girl.

"Have you ever used one like it?"

"No."

"Then why have you got it? Why did you bring it here, exposing your roommates and other girls to a thing like this?"

"I wanted to have it so I could learn how to use it."

"Oh, now really. You're not even a very good liar. Once again, where did you get it?"

"At a drug store in New York."

"You had to have a prescription from a doctor."

"Not where I bought it. I found out where my godmother got hers and they sold it to me without a prescription. He didn't care, the man that waited on me. A drug store in some hotel. I told him I'd bought one there before, and gave him my godmother's name. I don't know whether he looked it up or not. Maybe he did and maybe he didn't."

"How much did he charge you for it?"

"Twenty-five dollars. I think he overcharged me."

"And where did you get twenty-five dollars to spend on a thing like this?"

"I had it."

"Who gave it to you? Some man gave it to you."

"Yes."

"Who was the man?"

"If you're going to expel me I'm not going to tell you any more. I'm not going to get anyone else in trouble."

"No, you're in trouble enough yourself."

"So are you, Miss Roberts."

"I beg your pardon?"

"If you expel me, I'll commit suicide. Here at school. Don't think I'm bluffing, Miss Roberts. If you expel me I'll never get another scholarship."

"I'm quite certain of that," said Ida Roberts. "You don't deserve one."

"Yes I do. Look at my marks, look at my record. If you expel me for having one of those things, I'll kill myself."

"You're not the kind of girl that kills herself, not you."

"How do you know what kind of girl I am? Nobody knows what kind of girl I am. Maybe you'd like to know, but you don't."

"Just what are you implying there?" said Ida Roberts.

"You know what I'm implying. Look me straight in the eye and tell me you don't like me."

"As a matter of fact, I despise you," said Ida Roberts.

"You despise anybody that isn't rich, unless it happens to be Miss King. I know what's going on there, Miss Roberts."

"How did so much evil ever get concentrated in one young person? I must say I completely misjudged you, Marcy. I thought you were a common little thing, with some brains, but common. But I never for a minute suspected the amount of evil in you. I'm going to allow you to stay in school until your mother can get here to take you away. I suppose that would be two weeks at the most. I hope your father can come too."

"He can't. He's on maneuvers. But if you send for my mother, I'll be dead when she gets here. You can't have me watched twenty-four hours a day, every minute."

"I didn't say anything about having you watched," said Ida Roberts. "You have too much egotism to need that. Egotism and evil, I suppose it's not an unusual combination. I'll call a faculty meeting this morning, and this afternoon I'll write the letter to your mother."

"You are going to expel me?"

"The faculty committee usually follows my recommendations. Meanwhile nothing will be said to the student body. You'll continue to go to classes and meals and everything else as usual until your mother comes and takes you away."

"Remember what I said."

"I'll probably never forget anything that was said here today."

"Have you got a cigarette, Miss Roberts?"

"Don't be impudent, Marcy. And don't try my patience too far. You'll only make it more difficult to get in another school."

"Fuck school. Fuck it."

"Get out, please get out of my sight," said Ida Roberts. She got up and opened the door, held it open and looked away as the girl passed through. Then she returned to her chair and put her head on the desk and wept.

Shortly after two o'clock that afternoon smoke was discovered on the second floor of the dormitory, and by the time the engines arrived the fire had spread to the third floor. Firemen reported an unmistakable odor of cleaning fluid in various parts of the building. At about four o'clock, while the firemen were still fighting the fire in the dormitory, Marcy Bancroft was apprehended while sprinkling benzine on the cushions in the chapel. She was taken into custody and held without bail on a charge of felonious arson. The girls who lived in the dormitory were given refuge for the night at the homes of day students, and it was announced that the school would be closed down indefinitely.

The right forefinger stroked the right half of the moustache. "It could—it just possibly could—be a blessing in disguise." Grafton Williams was holding in check his enthusiasm for the idea that had just come to him. A terror, lasting not long enough to be sickening, struck Dorothy.

"A blessing in disguise? How?" said Dorothy.

They were in Grafton's office, two days after the destruction of the Hathaway dormitory. Grafton had sent for Dorothy and Joe Fuller, and Joe had not yet appeared. "I spoke to Joe this morning. He's going to be late. An emergency meeting of the Hathaway trustees, of which, as you know, he's one. Naturally they're all in a quandary.

The boarding students have literally no place to stay. There is some talk of putting cots in the gymnasium as a temporary measure. But already some of the parents have declared their intention of taking their daughters out of Hathaway and putting them in other schools. When you have over a hundred spirited young ladies, most of them from well-to-do families, you have a hundred major problems that have to be dealt with separately. The day students are a problem too, but girls like Lovey at least have a place to sleep. Getting the boarding girls into other schools at this time of year is going to be difficult. They haven't taken their mid-years yet, and the other schools are all preparing for their own mid-years. You can just imagine the pandemonium."

"I have five boarding girls at my house right now. I don't have to imagine it. They lost all their clothes and all their most precious possessions. But why is this a blessing in disguise?"

"I said it could be, from your point of view," said Grafton. "One thing the trustees are agreed upon, and that is that Hathaway *will* reopen. Not saying when, but whenever it can. Now I'm of the opinion that it may have to reopen as a somewhat smaller school, with the proportion of boarders to day pupils exactly reversed.

Two thirds day pupils, one third boarding. Let's say fifty day pupils and twenty-five boarders. And I have a scheme. But I had to discuss it with you before I broach it to Joe Fuller."

"Is your scheme the blessing in disguise?" said Dorothy.

"Yes," said Grafton. "Suppose we sell them your house and grounds, which would be about the right size for twenty-five boarders and seventy-five day pupils? Between now and next fall the necessary alterations could be made, if we get started right away."

"They could put up a new dormitory at Hathaway—"

"You haven't heard all of my scheme," said Grafton. "The other half depends on how persuasive I can be with our Catholic friends. You don't know Austin Fitz- gibbons, and no reason why you should, but I have always found him to be a man that I can sit down and talk to. We may not always see eye-to-eye on everything. We disagree violently on such matters as the depth for plant- ing certain roses, for instance. But he's always willing to hear what the other fellow has to say. Not as stubborn as some others of his breed. At all events, it occurred to me after my conversation with Joe Fuller that Hatha- way's misfortune *could* be, as I said, a blessing in dis- guise for you. Provided you'd be willing to turn over your house on very short notice. I think the Hathaway property would be perfect for the Catholic school, and what's more important, Austin Fitzgibbons might think so too."

"I wouldn't stand in the way," said Dorothy.

"Splendid," said Grafton. "It might also be a way for Joe Fuller to ease his conscience, too. You won't get a million for your property, but you'll get a good price. Fuller hasn't got the final say, but I can go before the Hathaway board and make them a very attractive proposition, with or without Fuller's cooperation. I don't mind telling you, in confidence, that Joe Fuller would like to be on certain boards that I'm on, and that he never in God's world will get on if I so much as blink a hesitant eye. And does he know it! He's been the picture of humility and discretion since that outburst a while ago. No Fuller has ever been on the board of the Wissahickon & Delaware Transportation Partnership, for instance."

"What on earth is the Wissahickon & Delaware Transportation Partnership? I've never heard of it," said Dorothy.

"Well, one of your uncles was on it. Your father died too young to be on it. I've been on it since I was forty-five."

"Is it a railway?"

"Yes, and no," said Grafton. "It was originally char-
tered as a railway and a canal system and a stagecoach
line. It never laid a foot of track, dug a cubic foot of
ditch, or bought so much as a set of harness. But it had
a great potentiality, what some men unkindly referred
to as a threat. In recent years it's become a dinner club,
but a dinner club with a difference. It meets six times
a year, and we feed ourselves magnificently, but before
we sit down to gorge ourselves we attend to business.
We usually have some say in what's going to happen in
Philadelphia transportation, but we don't limit ourselves
to that field. Informally, unofficially, we may decide who's
to be the next president of the University, or who's *not*.
We may discuss the advisability of widening certain
streets. There's darn little of importance that escapes
our notice. There are a lot of old Philadelphia names on
the board, but nobody gets on it by inheritance. Your
father-in-law was on it, but Billy wouldn't have got on
it if he'd lived to be a hundred. Unless, by some stretch
of the imagination, we decided to revive stagecoaches.
Then Billy's knowledge of horseflesh might have come
in handy. I'm joking, of course. Billy had no business
sense. Joe Fuller isn't going to make it either, but he
wants to and he might have if I hadn't discovered what
a crook he is. I'm plumping for Austin Fitzgibbons, but

it'll take a long time. The only Catholic in the Partnership, Reggie Keenan, looks down his nose at Austin. Reggie thinks Austin is coming up a little too fast, and I keep telling him it isn't a club. If it *were* a club, at least Austin's table manners are better than Reggie's. Reggie has reached that stage of self-assurance where he no longer makes any attempt to hide his gluttony. But I daresay Reggie one of these nights will choke on his second dozen Chincoteagues, and Austin will be duly elected to the Partnership."

"Reggie drinks a lot of port, too," said Dorothy.

"Yes," said Grafton. "Port, and sherry, and not averse to spirits. I'm prattling away in the hope that Fuller will turn up, but he may have to stay at his meeting for hours. Actually you don't have to be here when he arrives. It might even be better if you weren't. I'd like to get a quick decision out of him, and if you were here he might stall."

"Fine, I'll go," said Dorothy.

"Why were you shocked when I said this might be a blessing in disguise? Did you think me heartless and cruel?"

"I could never think that, Grafton," said Dorothy. "I don't know what was in my mind."

"Probably thought I was heartless and cruel without

realizing you were thinking it. Ah, well, in the practice
of law we sometimes tend to overlook the human equa-
tion. And yet the law is man's most civilized invention.
Religion is based on fear, medicine on pity. But the law
—oh, well. I hope you don't think this trip was a wild
goose chase."

Dorothy was home in time for lunch. Indeed, she was
home in time to put down the two brandies that she had
needed since Grafton Williams's opening remark. He had
been a name and face all her life, and in recent years a
name, face, and male friend of Billy's; but only since
Billy's death had he begun to seem capable of bleeding
if cut, of scratching if itched, of anger as well as indignation, of affection as well as approval. In a few months
he had become so humanized that he could have meant,
by the blessing in disguise, that he had somehow discovered the nature of her relations with Marcy Bancroft.
To speak of a blessing in disguise would have been his
way of approaching the subject. She had been needing
those two brandies for two hours, and she drank the
second slowly so that she would not need a third. She
brushed her teeth and gargled with mouthwash, and went
downstairs to do her duty as hostess to the displaced
girls from Hathaway.

One was from New York; one from Chicago; one from Indianapolis; one from Pasadena, California; one from Buffalo, New York. Their names all began with the letter B: the school had telephoned Dorothy and asked her how many girls she could give shelter to; she answered five, and five girls were assigned to Dorothy's house without regard to their compatibility or any other consideration than the fact that they were together on an alphabetical list. Baker, Baldwin, Ball, Barker, and Brockmyer. It occurred to Dorothy that Bancroft had been on the list between Ball and Barker, and she said as much. It turned out that none of the girls had liked Marcy, although none of them had ever had a serious quarrel with her. Lovey spoke up in a not very spirited defense of her recent house guest. "It's easy to say now that we never liked her," said Lovey. "But I can think of more unpopular girls at school." No one at the table was quite sure what had impelled Marcy to do the terrible thing she did, but they agreed that it could have been more terrible. She had picked a time when all the girls were out of the dormitory. If she had set the fires at night some of the girls surely would have been burned to death. They agreed that Marcy must have been taking revenge on the school, probably on Miss Roberts. Something must have been said or done during the conversation in Miss Roberts's office. Only the most serious kind of thing would have caused Miss Roberts to summon a girl to her office during classroom hours. The Indianapolis girl said she had *heard* that one of the dormitory biddies had found a missing wristwatch in Marcy's room. "I don't believe that for a minute," said Lovey. "Cigarettes, maybe, but not anything valuable." The Pasadena girl had a theory of her own, but she was not sure she wanted to say it in front of Mrs. Lewis.

"Go right ahead," said Dorothy.

"Well, I roomed with Marcy for one term, and if you ever roomed with her you found out that she had a habit of drawing strange pictures. She never showed them to anybody, but she didn't always tear them up. I and some of her other roommates saw them."

"Nasty pictures?" said Dorothy.

"Nasty, but more funny than nasty. They showed the upper half of a woman's body, with the lower half a man's. I know they sound awful, but they were really quite funny. Exaggerated. Maybe that's what the biddy found."

"The only one I ever saw wasn't very funny," said the Buffalo girl. "It was horrible, and she was hoping I'd see it, I know she was. She was a horrible girl, and we all felt sorry for her because she was supposed to be on scholarship. They shouldn't *have* scholarships at expensive schools like Hathaway. College, yes, but not at Hathaway and Miss Brandon's and places like that."

"They don't all set fire to the schools," said the New York girl.

"I didn't say they did. But they resent not having the things the other girls have and it makes them sour as swill. They ought to go to high school or less expensive boarding schools," said the Buffalo girl.

"That's why they call us snobs," said the New York girl.

"The real snobs are the girls that think high school isn't good enough for them, so they go to Hathaway and have a miserable time," said the Buffalo girl. "Then something like this happens."

"It isn't the girls that want to go to places like Hathaway. It's their parents that make them go," said the Indianapolis girl.

"But Marcy was a very good student, practically straight A's," said the New York girl.

"She had to to keep her scholarship so that she could go on and get another scholarship at college," said the

Buffalo girl. "Another thing. How would you like it if your parents sent you to school in September knowing they wouldn't see you again till June? Maybe they had their reasons. If your own parents don't want you home at Christmas there must be some good reason. Marcy would have been better off at a reform school—and that's probably where they'll send her, now."

There was silence.

"That's a horrible thought, Marcy in a reform school," said Lovey.

"Well, I should imagine her family could do something about that," said Dorothy. "Maybe it won't be reform school. I don't know what they do in a case like that, but I've never heard of a girl with Marcy's background going to the Protectory."

"Mummy, aren't *we* going to do anything about it?"

"No, we're not," said Dorothy.

"But you *liked* Marcy," said Lovey.

"I hardly knew her. She was only here three days. I let her have a few things of mine—"

"Yes, she was always trying on other girls' dresses," said the Buffalo girl. "That showed how miserable she was, not having things of her own. The trouble was, if you lent her a dress you had a hard time getting it back.

And if you lent her one thing she'd take others without asking. Last year she was going to visit some army people at Fort Niagara, and she asked me if she could stay at my house. Well, believe you me I got out of that in a jiffy. I didn't want my fifteen-year-old brother and his Nichols School friends coming across one of her drawings."

The conversation turned away from the topic of Marcy Bancroft and into a lively, detailed discussion of the several girls' losses in the fire. Dorothy did not take part in this discussion, but found herself glancing again and again at the Buffalo girl, her aristocratic bone structure, the set of her thin, delicate lips. An interesting girl, the girl from Buffalo.

Grafton Williams worked fast, a trait that was not outstanding in the reputation he had created for himself among laymen. It seemed to some of his clients that his pace was retarded by his fondness for unnecessary conversation, as though he had all the time in the world to go over ground already covered and ground that need not be covered at all. On his desk was a sterling silver set of postal scales which had belonged to his father, upon which someone had once remarked that they were essential equipment for a man who was never reckless with a two-cent stamp. The fact that the scales were decorative rather than useful did not affect the validity of the remark; Grafton was thorough and he was frugal.

His recreations—gardening and lawn tennis—committed him to no extravagances. He had worn the same white linen hat in both activities for twenty years, replacing the sweatband but not the hat itself. As the senior partner in Goodbody, Williams & Strayhorn, formerly Goodbody, Strayhorn & Goodbody, he occupied a carpeted corner office as big as a squash court. He accepted the quiet luxury and the size as suitable to the dignity of his position in the firm and the firm's position in the profession. He had a flat-top walnut desk where he conferred, and a roll-top desk where he worked alone, and the personal touches were a scale model of an 1800-type locomotive, a large photograph of his father in a Prince Albert, a slender silver vase in which occasionally stood a rose; a stuffed ruffed grouse, the official bird of the Commonwealth of Pennsylvania; a tall brass spittoon that had once belonged to Boies Penrose; a cut-glass jar that was always filled with hoarhound drops. Nothing had been moved from its original location. The usual calfbound legal volumes were kept out of sight, unfailingly returned to the law library down the hall after every use. "Ostentation in reverse," said Grafton Williams. "I want my clients to think I have it all up here," touching the side of his head. It was ostentation in reverse that had kept him from shaving off his moustache when they began to go out of style.

"It's all agreed," he said to Dorothy. "And having said that, I must also add that nothing is settled, officially. But I know you'll be greatly relieved to hear that the Catholics are going to buy Hathaway, and Hathaway is going to buy your place. Not a thing down on paper. No signatures. No earnest-money. But it's the kind of deal that I like best, although as a lawyer I should deplore it, because if such transactions became common, a lot of my colleagues would be in difficulties. Some of them would be selling neckties at Wanamaker's."

"How perfectly marvelous, Grafton. You did both things?" said Dorothy.

"They intertwined, so to speak. First I spoke to my friend Austin Fitzgibbons, and when I got his word that the Catholics were ready to make an offer for Hathaway, I spoke to Joe Fuller. I was less candid with him. I told him I had a buyer for Hathaway, conditional on Hathaway's taking over your place. The idea appealed to him in principle, as I knew it would. Certain other trustees of Hathaway are just about ready to close the school for good, but Joe likes being trustee of Hathaway. It carries a small amount of prestige and a minimum of work on his part. Understandably, he was curious to know who'd buy Hathaway, but I wouldn't tell him until I had his word that Hathaway would buy your house. An oral agreement of that kind is binding in some cases and sometimes not, but it was in this case because if I say that Joe Fuller agreed to it, my word would stand up against Joe Fuller's denial. It pays to have a reputation for probity."

"And you have that," said Dorothy.

"I have," said Grafton. "It then became a question of money, and it's still a question of money. But Hathaway is going to get enough money from the Catholics to buy your place and have a little left over. I couldn't give all these details to Joe Fuller because in his tactless way he might charge in and upset the apple-cart. The key figure in this whole transaction is Austin Fitzgibbons, and to put it mildly, Fuller rubs him the wrong way. To put it extremely mildly. On the other hand, Fitzgibbons trusts me. Although I seem to be acting as entrepreneur, I shall charge no fee to Fitzgibbons and the Catholics, as entrepreneuer, since I am acting in the interest of my client, you. It would be entirely ethical for me to send them a bill, and Austin knows that, but he also knows that I'm the lawyer for Billy's estate. The Jews have a saying,

'One hand washes the other,' that expresses it nicely. So there we are, Dorothy. The work is done. It may sound very unbusiness-like to you, but I assure you that you'll come out all right financially."

"How much?" said Dorothy.

He smiled. "I think you'll get about $400,000. But don't let your imagination run away with you. You won't have $400,000 to spend. You'll have legal expenses, including our fee. And then you'll want to buy a house to live in. We're a long way from the million I'd like to have extracted from Joe Fuller, but I've respected your wishes in that matter."

"Thank you."

"Not to be self-congratulatory about this, but I think you have reason to be proud of me. I'm pretty pleased with myself."

"All right, I'll give you a kiss," said Dorothy.

"Not at our age, Dorothy."

"*Our* age? I like that!"

"Past adolescence, Dorothy," said Grafton. "Not that we probably couldn't learn a thing or two from the adolescents of today."

There it was again, the accidental *double entendre* by this naïve and crafty man, and Dorothy responded out of her guilty knowledge of herself. "I daresay we could," she said. "Half the time I don't even know what's going on in my own daughter's mind."

"If you know half the time you're doing very well," said Grafton. "Now I'd like to play uncle for a moment or two, Dorothy, if I have your permission."

"Go right ahead," she said.

"Don't you think it's time you had a change of scenery, gave yourself a rest? I've been on the verge of saying this half a dozen times, but there was no point in getting you to go away before things were settled. You'd go away, and then I'd have to bring you back. But now you can go and stay as long as you like. Get entirely away from Philadelphia, your house, your well-meaning friends, me. You've been under a constant strain since Billy died, but instead of getting better it's gotten worse. Has anyone else noticed it besides me?"

"If they have they haven't said anything," said Dorothy.

"You've been a widow for nearly eight months, and you're still a young and attractive woman. Do you see what I'm driving at? If I knew you better, or not at all, I could say it more easily. Dorothy, you need a man."

"You mean to sleep with?" said Dorothy.

"Yes, I do mean that, among other things. It surprises you, coming from me. It's more the kind of thing Joe

Fuller would say, and I'm sure Joe wouldn't have to look very far to suggest the man. But he's not the man, or anyone like him. And needless to say, neither am I. So we rule out two possibilities. I suggest a trip where you will meet someone new, who'll be attentive to you, and you can be—attentive—in return. Even if it's only a shipboard romance, Dorothy. But I'm hoping it'll turn into something more permanent. This is dangerous advice, I know. But you have no idea how many times you've sat here and yet been a thousand miles away. Other times it seemed to me that you were on the verge of giving in to an emotional outburst, to blow off steam. Have I said too much?"

"No, what you say is all true," said Dorothy.

"I don't for a moment believe that sex is the best or the only answer. Nevertheless—well, to be deprived of it after eighteen years of married life with a vigorous man like Billy—that's a major upset in anyone's life."

"You're the last man I'd have said ever gave much thought to sex," said Dorothy.

"I think about it all the time. Maybe that's why I'm a good husband. I've never slept with anyone but my own wife, but that hasn't kept me from an insatiable curiosity about other people. There's a world of difference between that and philandering. I'd make the world's worst philanderer, but you'd be positively amazed to know how much thought and study I've given the subject. You've heard of Freud, Sigmund Freud?"

"Yes," she said.

"I could pass an examination on the writings of Freud, Havelock Ellis. There's a man out at the University, Dr. Polzer, Karl Polzer. We have dinner together once a month. He uses me as a guinea pig, a seventh generation American, and I in turn use him as my tutor. The questions he asks me are perfectly outrageous, but he puts me in a good mood because he sounds like Weber & Fields. I tell him absolutely everything he wants to know. He told me some interesting things about you—"

"*Me?*"

"He doesn't even know your name, but he wanted to know all about the women I see. Family. Clients. Servants."

"And what did he say about me?"

"That you were frustrated and had probably reached a critical point in your life. He asked me if you had reached the menopause, and he was quite disappointed when I wasn't able to answer him."

"For your information, not yet. But I don't know much about it. He thinks I ought to go away?"

"He didn't say so in so many words," said Grafton.

"He wouldn't make a recommendation without knowing more about you. But *I* think you ought to go away."

"So do I," said Dorothy.

"Then what's stopping you?" said Grafton.

"Nothing, now," she said. "Well, Lovey."

Dearest Mummy:

Three schools in one year! A good thing I don't have to be properly educated or else we would have to give it up as a bad job. They don't even use the same books that I used at Hathaway & H. did not use the same books as Brandon's. But so far I like this place better than the others. (Not saying much.) My room is on the top floor & can look out & see nothing but trees, trees, trees. Mountains, mountains, mountains. The girls are more similar to the girls at Brandon's than Hathaway and fewer. I dread to think what this must be costing you. The food is better than the other places, also the rooms are better furnished, that is more cheerful and not so much like a convent. The teachers are good, bad & indifferrent, just like most schools. The days are very warm but because of being in the mountains it gets very cold at night. There is not much more to say so I will bring to a close this witty, interesting letter. Do not worry about me. I will not run away from this school, besides it would not be as easy as the time I ran away from Brandon's. Also have no place to go until you get the new house.

Love,

Lovey

P.S.: Almost forgot to tell you that while walking through the gym last week I stopped to look at some of the school pictures. There was one in particular that attracted my attention, a picture of the school Horse Show taken in 19??. The man giving the cup for All Around Best Rider (a girl named Finley) looked very familiar. No wonder! It was Daddy! "Presented by F. Willingham Lewis." It was the only time I cried since I have been here, he looked so young and healthy.

L.

P.S. Later: Just found out that the "girl" who won the cup is the same Miss Finley who teaches Latin here. You would never think to look at her that it was the same "girl."

L.

Lovey dear:

Thank you for all your letters. I was delighted to get them and I do appreciate your interesting descriptions of life at school. This is the first opportunity I have had to write you but will try to do better in the future.

This is a delightful place to rest. I must have needed this rest as I did practically nothing but sleep the first week I was here. The Inn is not very far from Saratoga Springs, where your father and I used to visit when we were first married, but the racing season has not begun and in any case I did not come here for excitement. Dr. and Mrs. Walters, who own the Inn, are a charming host and hostess, not the over-friendly type that you might expect. There is no one here I ever saw before, which makes it just right for me. There is a 9-hole golf course and three clay courts. I have gotten in a little tennis with Dr. and Mrs. Walters and one of the other guests. I swim at least once a day in the indoor pool, sometimes twice. Most of the other guests are somewhat older than I so I have practically all the facilities to myself. In the evening I usually play bridge or read, depending on how tired I get during the day. I would not care to stay here forever but it is a perfect place to relax and get a lot of fresh air. I will be here until a week from Monday, then back to Philadelphia to stay with the Williamses while looking for a house. I am thinking of renting a house for the summer until I find the right one to buy. I am very glad you like it where you are as that settles the school problem for next year. After that we might go abroad for a year. How would you like that? We could take a house somewhere and you would have a chance to use your French, etc. If you should change your mind about wanting to go to college we would have to forget about going abroad, but we can discuss that this summer. I never had the slightest desire to go to college but things have changed since I was that age.

Will write to you from the Williams' if not before.

Your loving
Mummy

Dear Lovey:

I suggest that you postpone reading this letter until you have an opportunity to read it undisturbed by outside interruptions.

It is difficult to know where to begin. The fact is that your mother has had a slight nervous breakdown and will remain at Dr. Walters' past the time she had planned to come to our house. The effect on your schedule will be that you will come to our house and stay with us until your mother is able to join you. I have spoken to your headmistress and to Miss Finley (who knew your father and mother years ago) as well as to other parties concerned and all are agreed that the sensible course is for you to finish out the term and come here from school.

Naturally you will want to know about your mother. No doubt you were aware that she has been under a strain since your father died. It became noticeable to me in the course of our meetings in my office that she was inclined to become easily distracted, while at other times she appeared to be in a highly nervous state with no apparent cause. I suggested that she spend a few weeks at Dr. Walters', but my suggestion was made too late. Dr. Walters informed me by telephone that your mother had lapsed into a state of depression that while not extremely serious, justified her having twenty-four-hour care for several days. During that time she could not remember who she was, which is one of the usual symptoms of a person undergoing a mild breakdown.

I must emphasize that there is no cause for alarm. Your mother has responded to Dr. Walters' treatment and as soon as I receive word from him that she is her old self again, you will be able to visit her. Meanwhile we are looking forward to having you with us.

> Affectionately,
> Grafton Williams

Dear Mr. Williams:

Thank you for your check in amount of $865.50 in payment of our statement up to and including June 30.

As I told you over the telephone, Mrs. Lewis is coming along nicely but is not yet ready to resume residence at home or to have visitors. We believe that until she expresses the desire to return to Philadelphia and the routine of daily existence, it would be unwise for her to leave. A premature return to everyday life could have an undesirable effect. The desire to return must originate with her.

Mrs. Lewis is now fully aware that we have been

treating her for a nervous collapse. She has not, however, shown any signs of wishing to cooperate with us in the treatment. She has refused to answer questions regarding her personal life. This lack of cooperation, while not helpful to us, is not unusual in such cases and sometimes indicates a strong instinct for self-preservation that is by no means an unhealthy sign. Many women have breakdowns at home that are no less serious than Mrs. Lewis' but are not treated, owing to the reluctance of the women's families to admit that such things occur. I would remind you once again that it is our policy here to maintain a rest home and not an institution for more advanced cases of mental disturbance; therefore at the first indication that Mrs. Lewis has become a more advanced case, we would notify you immediately so that she could be removed to an institution that is prepared to treat such cases. However, it does not seem necessary at this time to request her removal. In my opinion, such removal at this time might do more harm than good to the patient. You may, if you wish, send a qualified physician here for consultation with me. But here again, I seriously question the desirability of such a step, in view of the possible effect on the patient. Mrs. Lewis knows why she is here and it does not disturb her that I know why she is here. But she does not wish others to know, although I felt it my duty to inform you of the true nature of the case.

I wish to further point out to you that we have had similar cases here. Many patients return here voluntarily to escape from certain realities. We feel that we are performing a useful service by providing a refuge for such men and women.

Very truly yours,

S. S. Walters, M.D.

Dear Grafton:

I have read the letter from S. S. W. Unfortunately I am unable to meet with you to discuss it in person as I leave tonight for New York and am sailing from Hoboken, N.J., tomorrow for my meetings in Berlin, Vienna and Switzerland. I shall be gone five weeks before resuming my work at the University. "The bus-man's holiday," as it is called.

S. S. W.'s degree is from a good medical school (I

checked up on him to that extent). I should be interested to learn something of his accomplishments in the business world. Forgive this cheap sarcasm. It is not a crime for a doctor to make money. Never the less, the evidence which I discern from his letter compels me to stand in admiration of his business acumen whilst standing less in admiration of his conduct as a physician. Much of what he says is true: (1) instinct for self-preservation, (2) breakdowns in the privacy of the home, (3) desirability of casting the patient out in the cruel world of reality. But I do not like to think of the consequences of "treating her for nervous collapse" from such an incomplete history of the case.

You ask my opinion, I give it to you. S. S. W. maintains a tennis-golf club for homosexuals and others who are in need of more serious therapy. We have no record of the patients who did not return to his club voluntarily or otherwise. I should hazard a guess that many of his patients depart from his club after a few weeks' rest with their consciences clear, confident that when they get into trouble again they have a refuge from the consequences. I shall say nothing of those patients who sincerely wanted help but did not get it.

I shall now desert you to drink some decent beer but

your friend's problem will be in my thoughts.

Your devoted friend,

Karl

P.S.: Be careful. You are getting in deep.

The Williamses had been very nice to her. They had brought up children of their own—sons, now gone from home, but it was a house in which young people had lived and to which they and their children would return. Johnny, John Grafton Williams, was at the moment working as a dude wrangler on a ranch in Montana; Buddy, Richard Grafton Williams, was cruising in New England waters with his wife, a last holiday before beginning his interneship in a Boston hospital. "Good boys, both of them," Grafton Williams would say, as pleased with Johnny, who was not sure what he wanted to do, as with Buddy, who was very sure what he wanted to do. "I think Johnny wants to be a writer, but he's too shy to say so," said Grafton Williams. "I was a little disappointed when he said he didn't want to study law. I tried to persuade him to go to law school while he was making up his mind. After all, he'd be using his brains, and a law degree is a nice thing to have even if you have no intention of practicing. But his answer to that was that he didn't want to think like a lawyer. I asked him what he meant by that and he said that a lawyer has a disciplined mind, you get used to thinking according to rules, precedents, and that wasn't the way he wanted his mind to work. Then I discovered that he had written a novel in college. He never showed it to me or to his mother, wouldn't talk about it, and wasn't at all pleased with it, but was a little pleased that he had finished. I don't know what the subject matter was, and I didn't press him to tell me. He's getting thirty dollars a month and his keep at the ranch. When that's over he's going to look for a job. He can stay on the ranch if he cares to. The owner has a working ranch and there's plenty for Johnny to do, but he doesn't care for the idea of a winter in Montana."

"I don't think I would either," said Lovey.

"My guess is that the next stop will be Europe, Asia, or South America. He's had jobs every summer since he went to college. Hard work, the first summer. I doubt if you'd remember when he came home that summer. All this friends were brown as berries, but Johnny was pale and thin from two months in a steel mill. We were afraid he might be getting tuberculosis."

"How *awful,*" said Lovey.

"But he wasn't. We fattened him up before he went back to college, and by the end of sophomore year he'd attained his full growth. Six-one, a hundred and eighty pounds, almost made the varsity crew and did make it junior year. Then didn't go out for it senior year. He rowed, but only for exercise, not for glory. It didn't contribute much to his popularity, going out on the Charles River all by himself and resting on his oars while the galley slaves were slaving."

"Did he care what they thought?" said Lovey.

"Not one bit," said Grafton Williams. "Some of their fathers blamed me. They tried to tell me that it was my duty to see to it that Johnny rowed for Harvard. I didn't see it that way. I've never believed that there was any such obligation. I actually discouraged him from going out for football, which he played in prep school. If he wanted to row, that was all right, but only if he wanted to. Not because he owed anything to Harvard—and it wasn't to Harvard. It was to a few old men like me who liked to crow it over Yale. I won against Yale, in singles and in doubles, but I'm sure it didn't make the slightest difference to A. T. Hadley or to A. L. Lowell."

"Are they the ones you beat?"

"They were the presidents of Yale and Harvard, respectively. So, my Johnny has his varsity letter and some other letters that came in the mail from elderly soreheads. I have my varsity letter for winning against Yale, and some letters from the same soreheads. While Buddy, who never got a letter at Harvard, is undoubtedly the most admired of the three of us. I hope it all makes sense to you. It doesn't to me."

"It makes a lot of sense, all of it. You all three did what you wanted to do, and when Johnny's ready again, he'll do what he wants to do again."

"I think so, whatever that may be," said Grafton Williams. "Of course you believe in doing what you want to do."

"I don't believe in doing what other people say you ought to do," said Lovey.

"But when you happen to want to do what people say you ought to do, you don't go against what you want to do merely to maintain your independence?"

"That wouldn't be very independent, would it?" said Lovey.

"No, but I was sounding you out," said Grafton

Williams. "You see, there's a possibility that you may be faced with an important decision, and when you make it I don't want you to be influenced by any outside considerations."

"It has something to do with Mummy?" said Lovey.

"Yes, but not entirely. It has at least as much to do with you, your life, your future. I'm very glad you took French leave of Miss Brandon's last fall. Not that I entirely approve of what you did, but it *was* an important decision, and you made it on your own. It took courage and independence. Much more courage and independence than it took Johnny to give up the Harvard crew. If no more, certainly as much."

"What's the decision you want me to make now?"

"Not this minute, not today. But in the not too distant future, Lovey, you may have to decide whether you want to live with us or with your mother. Naturally your immediate reaction is the obvious one. You want to live with your mother. But is that because you want to, or because you feel you have to? And would you feel you had to because that's what you ought to feel, what other people expect you to feel? It could take a lot more courage to come and live with us than to live with your mother, and it could be the thing that you really wanted to do."

"Is Mummy that bad?" said Lovey.

"I can't say, I don't know. If you were my flesh and blood, which of course you are, distantly. Your grandmother Lewis was a cousin of my grandfather Grafton's, so we have the usual Philadelphia kinship. But if you were closer, if you were my niece, I could go to court as next of kin and get permission to have you appointed my ward. I'm a bit hazy on the law, but something like that could be done."

"Then she *is* that bad?" said Lovey.

"Well, I didn't say I *was* going to court, Lovey. It's always better to stay out of court if you can. Those things get on the record, and years later there they are for anyone to see. Actually the last thing I want to do is go to court. But the last thing I want to see happen to you just now is for you to live with your mother."

"Why don't you want to tell me what's wrong with her?" said Lovey. "What are you keeping from me that's so awful?"

Both thumb and forefinger pressed the moustache. "To all appearances, nothing is wrong with her. She's not, uh, peculiar, as they say. She doesn't talk to herself, or foam at the mouth, or any of those things that the mentally disturbed are noted for. But she has shown certain tendencies in her behavior that I'm sure no one ever knew about. I know I didn't, and I have quite a collection of information regarding people's behavior, people we know."

"Does she misbehave morally?" said Lovey.

"That would be one way of putting it."

"In other words, it has to do with sex?" said Lovey.

"Yes, it has."

"But I knew that," said Lovey.

"Oh, now, you couldn't have, Lovey."

"But I did. I saw her one time, in a certain person's car. I was up on the roof of the stable, where I wasn't supposed to be, and I saw them. I thought she was asleep, but she wasn't."

"You don't have to tell me any more about it. You were sure it was your mother? It couldn't have been anyone else?"

"It was Mr. Fuller. It made me so dizzy I had to hold on to the top of the roof to keep from falling off."

"How old were you then?"

"Eleven or twelve. After that I used to spy on her every time Mr. Fuller came to our house. I was going to tell Daddy. But that was the only time I ever saw her, or them. But it was Mummy, all right."

"Well, let's not talk about it any more."

"I heard of girls at school doing it because they were afraid to have babies."

"I'd really rather not talk about it, Lovey. You're what, sixteen?"

"Seventeen."

"Still too young to know about such things, but I must say you've made it easier for me to explain why you ought to be away from your mother for a while."

"Why? Does she go around doing that to strange men?"

"No. But her moral sense is deadened. She isn't responsible for her behavior. That's the way I look at it now."

"But good grief, Mr. Williams! I know girls that do that, and they're not even in love with the boys. Girls my age and even younger. And Mummy's a married woman. How do you know it wasn't Mr. Fuller's fault?"

"Seventeen," said Grafton Williams. "You haven't made it much easier for me after all, Lovey."

"Oh, there's more?"

"Yes, there's more. And I'm going to have to tell you. Did you know any girls at school that had that kind of relation with each other?"

"Yes I did, and if you say Mummy did, you're a liar. A damn liar!"

"I'm not a liar, Lovey."

"How would you know? Who'd ever tell you a thing like that? You're making this up and I don't know why. I know why. Mummy turned you down, so you make up this filthy, disgusting lie. I want to get out of this house and never come back again."

He was silent.

The girl, silent for a moment, suddenly jumped to her feet and shouted, "It's a lie, a dirty filthy lie, I tell you! You're the worst man I ever knew."

"That part I agree with," said Grafton Williams. "I never felt worse in my life."

Lovey moved to the telephone on his desk, and gave a number which he recognized as Joe Fuller's. "It's no use," said Grafton. "Mr. and Mrs. Fuller are both away. And why do you want to talk to them?"

"To get away from this house," said Lovey.

"And tell them what a scoundrel I am, and why?"

"Yes."

"Don't do that, young woman," said Grafton. "Mrs. Williams and I have kept your mother's secret. It would be very foolish of you to spread it around." He went to the hall door and called his wife.

She entered the study, looked from one to the other, and Grafton nodded. "I had to tell her," he said.

"The whole story?" said Gay Williams.

"No, but the thing I didn't want to tell her," said Grafton.

"Didn't want to tell me? That's another lie," said Lovey.

"Lovey, Mr. Williams told you about your mother because I was too much of a coward to. I couldn't bear to. Grafton, you leave us for a little while, please."

"I'll be on the side porch," said Grafton, and left.

"Oh, dear," said Gay Williams. "You don't *know* what a good man that is. You can't know how you hurt him with that accusation. He wouldn't lie to save his life. And if you knew how he dreaded having to tell you about your mother. It was my job to do, but I wasn't equal to it. Sit down over there, Lovey, and stop muttering those words. If you have to say shit, say it. I've never said it before in my whole life, and I hope I never say it again. But I don't like muttering. Light a cigarette, if you care to."

"I don't care to," said Lovey.

"Then don't," said Gay Williams. "We've tried to make you comfortable here, as comfortable as possible under the circumstances. But there are limits, and calling Grafton Williams a liar is one of them. No matter how upset you are, you're old enough now to behave as a mature person, especially toward a man who couldn't have done more for you if you'd been his own daughter. It's time someone told you, for instance, that Mr. Williams has spent months trying to improve your mother's and your financial affairs. No one else could have done what he's done for you. Thanks entirely to him, you and your mother have financial security, far beyond anything anyone could expect or hope for. You're old enough now not to take those things for granted. They don't just happen, and you'll never know just how lucky you were to have had him and not someone else in charge of your father's estate. You probably don't know the first thing about money matters, but you're going to have to learn. You don't want to talk about money. Of course not, and neither do I, and I wasn't going to, but the very thought of the slightest doubt on my husband's integrity makes me very cross. He is the soul of honor, whether it's a financial matter or anything else. In your blundering, youthful way you struck a foul blow, and you should be spoken to about it. Very well. I've made my point."

Lovey lit a cigarette.

"Now I'm going to have to talk to you about your mother," said Gay Williams. "It was cruel of me to shirk my responsibility, to pass that on to my husband. I remember hearing from both your mother and your father how eager you were to grow up, to be treated as a mature person. Well, maturity has been thrust upon you by one thing and another. Life has a way of giving you just what you want, or think you want, and maturity was what you wanted. Do you like it? Whether you like it or not, there it is. Your father's tragic death, your running away from school—I never knew why—and your mother's nervous breakdown. And I'm sure there have been other things, even before your father died, and since. What Mr. Williams didn't understand was that he should have *insisted* on my being the one to talk to you about your mother. I shirked it because it was too unpleasant, but he should have insisted. A woman can be more outspoken with another woman than she ever can be with a man. Just the mere fact that one of them is a man and the other is a woman creates a certain awkwardness, and when the man is in middle age and the woman is a young girl— well, that makes it even worse. So he should have insisted, and *I* should have insisted on being the one to talk to you. Never does any good to shirk. And now, thanks to my shirking, we have to have this talk in an atmosphere of hostility."

The girl crushed her half-smoked cigarette and lit another.

"I don't know how old I was when I first knew about

women having relations with other women, but I know
that by the time I got to Bryn Mawr I'd heard about it
more than once. Four years at Bryn Mawr, and I still
wasn't sure what they did. I pretended to know, because
we were very sophisticated at Bryn Mawr, but I didn't
actually know. Then that summer I did find out, traveling
with three other girls in a third-class cabin. I was hor-
rified. They had picked me to go along as the fourth
because they thought I was one of them. My false
sophistication. That was the worst week I ever spent in
my entire life. I pretended I was seasick, but that didn't
do any good. They just went on, paying no attention to
me, but quarreling and making love among themselves.
I'm telling you this awful story because I want you to
know that I've had some experience with women like that.
A whole week of it. I could never tell you all that went
on in that tiny stateroom. I've never told anyone, not
even my husband. Cruel, jealous, degenerate people, none
of them now living in Philadelphia, thank heaven."

Lovey crushed out another cigarette, lit another.

"Do I think your mother is like that? Yes, I do," said
Gay Williams. "Lovey, your mother was arrested last
week in Buffalo, New York. A Mrs. Baldwin complained
to the police that your mother had been annoying her

daughter. It was kept out of the papers, because Mrs. Baldwin refused to prosecute, but only because the girl is a friend of yours."

"Iris Baldwin," said Lovey. "Where is Mummy now?"

"She's back at Dr. Walters'. But now she's getting special care. She can't leave the grounds without an attendant. She may be there for a long time, or she may have to be moved to a sanitarium. The whole burden has been on Mr. Williams' shoulders up to now, but a doctor is going up from New York, and if he advises a sanitarium, she'll be taken there."

"My mother is crazy, is that it?" said Lovey.

"No, not crazy, Lovey. But far from well."

"I'm not as surprised as I ought to be, I guess," said Lovey. "And it's a little better that they can find some excuse. Iris Baldwin. The Duchess, some of us called her. The Duchess of Buffalo. The strange thing is that I always thought Iris was a little that way."

"Maybe she was," said Gay Williams.

As of the Middle 1920s the Childs family could, if need be, boast of a long and distinguished participation in the history of New Jersey. In the War of the Revolution one ancestor, Isaac Childs, was brevetted a brigadier by

George Washington himself. Isaac, a prosperous farmer and one of the last in New Jersey to own slaves, had been unconvinced of the justice of the Continental cause, but after the Battle of Trenton he underwent a change of heart. Accompanied by the younger of his two sons he rode thirty miles on horseback to offer his support to General Washington, and the offer was accepted immediately. A week later two Hessian deserters appeared at the Childs farm. Owing to the confusion of tongues they were unable to give a satisfactory explanation of their visit, and when they refused to leave, John Childs shot and killed one of the Hessians with his pistol. The second Hessian thereupon broke John's skull with a carpenter's mallet and left him to die on the barn floor. When word of the tragedy reached Isaac he was excused from further military duty and, with his surviving son, returned to the farm to find that his two unmarried field hands had run away.

In subsequent generations the Childs family produced a governor of New Jersey, another governor who resigned to fill out an unexpired term in the United States Senate; two trustees of the College of New Jersey at Princeton; an ambassador to the Netherlands, and various colonels, full commanders, and masters of fox hounds.

One of the colonels shot and killed his wife when he found her in bed with the family physician, whom he shot but did not kill. The second master of fox hounds was found not guilty of statutory rape upon the daughter of a harnessmaker in Far Hills. Another colonel won a suit for libel against the publisher of a Newark newspaper, but never lived down the publisher's charge that he had bribed the members of a legislative committee during an investigation of certain streetcar franchises in Camden. At least once in every decade since 1750 the citizens of New Jersey were given cause to celebrate or deplore the activities of the Childs family. In 1925 Sky Childs became the first player to make the Walter Camp and Grantland Rice All-America football teams. His football reputation helped him at home when in 1926 he accidentally shot and killed Captain the Honourable T. A. B. Flaxham during a tiger hunt in India. In the same year he eloped with Lovey Lewis on the night he first met her.

Sky, who was not unmindful of his bride's standing in Philadelphia, easily persuaded her to retain the house on the Main Line, and Lovey, who was in the first raptures of love, was more than willing to change her mind about the house. "We'll keep the house," said Sky. "I can afford it." The fact that they took a *pied-à-terre* in New York, spent more of their time there and never belonged to Philadelphia society, was of small consequence.

Virginia Vernon, the sobsister who covered the elopment for the *Daily News*, declared that Sky and Lovey were made for each other: the wealthy sportsman-millionaire, the society heiress, and love at first sight, the midnight dash to Elkton, Maryland; the union of two prominent families. If they were not made for each other, they were made for the tabloid press. Irving Berlin and Ellin Mackey had settled down, and a new romance was needed to diversify reader interest in a period when circulation figures rose and fell with news of Leonard Kip Rhinelander and Ruth Jones, Ruth Snyder and Judd Gray, and the Hall-Mills case in New Jersey. Sky and Lovey, Lovey and Sky. Sky punched a fresh guy at the Central Park Casino; Lovey sailed for Europe without Sky but changed her mind and left the ship by tugboat before it reached open water. Sky announced plans to fly the Atlantic before young Lindbergh could beat him to it. Lovey declined an offer to appear in a Ziegfeld revue. Sky was suspended from the Racquet & Tennis Club for bringing a live monkey to the bar. Lovey was arrested for speeding on the Jericho Turnpike. Sky and Lovey were dropped from the Social Register. Sky disrupted the opening ceremonies of the National Horse Show by riding a mule into the arena during the playing of the national anthem. Lovey announced that she was going to volunteer to work for the election of Alfred E. Smith. Sky announced that he would seek the Republican nomination for governor. Blind items in the gossip columns reported and contradicted rumors that Lovey was having a romance with an orchestra leader and that Sky bought a diamond bracelet for a showgirl who belonged to a notorious racketeer.

The blind items were comparatively few in number. Lovey and Sky, Sky and Lovey were photogenic, and the editors preferred, stories that could be accompanied by pictures. When nothing else was happening to pep up the tabloid pages an editor would send a feature writer to ask Lovey Childs what she thought of American men versus the titled foreigners who came here looking for eligible heiresses. "It seems to be a thriving business," Lovey replied to one reporter, and the reporter could go on from there. The publicity that Lovey and Sky got was neither sought nor resisted by them; they were not movie stars, they had no paid hand to tip off the city desks or to put pressure on the publishers to play up or kill a story. They were an accident of timing between murders and divorces, a young and physically attractive couple whose behavior was unconventional without being purposefully defiant. They were of the same genre as Jimmy Walker, without the ominous Tammany Hall and the frowning Roman Catholic hierarchy as threatening spoilsports. Sky was "the playboy," Lovey was "the madcap," and New York adored them until they changed the character that had been invented for them.

It was in character for Lovey to say she liked Al Smith, and for Sky to pretend that his answer to such heresy would be to run for governor of New Jersey. It was inevitable, too, that two such people should attract and be attracted to an orchestra leader and a gangster's moll. So far Sky and Lovey were observing a convention of the unconventionality of their set. But it was not permissible for Lovey or Sky to behave in such a manner as to require the tabloid readers to take them seriously. They had become public entertainers, as much so in effect as though they held cards in Actors Equity, and when Sky was named in a paternity suit by a telephone operator at a Broadway hotel, the serious side of the fun-loving life was exposed. According to the testimony, Sky checked in at the hotel with a chorus girl from a night club, registered as Captain and Mrs. John Smith (in print the fact that he called the girl Pocahontas did not seem very funny), and remained at the hotel after the chorus girl departed at noon the next day. He sent a bellboy to a 49th Street speakeasy for a quart of Scotch, and in the course of making various telephone calls invited the operator to have lunch in his room. She accepted the invitation, and he behaved like a perfect gentleman until it was time for her to return to her switchboard. He pleaded with her not to leave him alone, threatening to jump out the window if she did, and promised her that he would use his influence with the manager to protect her job if she would spend the afternoon with him. Thus persuaded, she stayed, and had relations with him twice during the afternoon. He checked out of the hotel before dinner, and she heard no more from him until a week later, when he asked her to meet him at a friend's apartment. She agreed, and went to a small apartment on West 55th Street where she again had relations with him. She denied that she also had relations with his friend who rented the apartment, but admitted that the friend was present during her relations with Sky. Yes, she had taken a few drinks. Yes, all three had disrobed. No, it was not possible that she had had relations with both men. But was it not true that she had remained in the apartment after Sky left, and was it not true that she *then* had relations with Sky's friend? Was it not also true that a third man came to the apartment and that she had had relations with him as well? Was it not, in fact, true that she had telephoned a girl friend to join her at the apartment and that she and the girl friend had committed several unnatural acts with each other and were paid the sum of fifty dollars apiece before leaving the apartment? Was it not true that the plaintiff had been given a suspended sentence in New London, Connecticut, on a charge of prostitution during a Harvard-Yale boat race and that she made it a practice to prey upon young men whose families were well-to-do? Had she not listened in on the defendant's conversation with the speakeasy proprietor, thereby gaining information as to the defendant's true identity, and did she not then invite herself to his room for the purpose of solicitation? Was it not arithmetically as well as biologically possible that the father of her child could have been any of several dozen men? "You're a God damn liar," she shouted to the defense attorney.

The trial lasted from Monday to Friday. The *Daily News* and the *Daily Mirror* appeared on Sunday night with identical lines on the front page: "LOVEY LOYAL!" She attended every session of the trial, seated beside Sky, "impassive through her ordeal, but giving silent testimony of her devotion to the subdued playboy." They spoke of her aristocratic bearing, her thoroughbred manner, her ill-disguised scorn for the woman whose charges (according to Virginia Vernon) had put an

ugly ending to the sparkling story of the adventures of
Lovey and Sky. Miss Vernon's remark, appearing in the
Thursday paper, was prophetic: the jury brought in
its verdict at 3:10 Friday afternoon, and Sky was free
to go, which he did—alone. Miss Vernon, covering the
women's angle, stayed close to Lovey as she left the
courtroom. "What will you do now, Lovey?" said Virginia. "Do you and Sky have any plans?"

"He must have had some, he left so quickly," said
Lovey.

"I see. You're not going to meet him later? You were
so loyal, coming here every day, I thought maybe you'd
have plans for a second honeymoon."

"Maybe he has, but it won't be with me," said Lovey.

"Oh? Are you going to leave him? You two splitting
up?" said Virginia.

"I guess you'll have to draw your own conclusions,
Miss Vernon," said Lovey.

"In other words, I wouldn't be wrong if I said that
you *are* splitting up?"

"You saw him leave."

"And you don't know where he went?"

"I haven't the faintest idea," said Lovey.

"But you've been living with him while he was out

on bail, at the Park Avenue apartment," said Virginia
Vernon. "You and he and the lawyer left together every
afternoon."

"They very kindly dropped me at 760 Park. I don't
know where they went from there."

"This is quite a story you've given me, Lovey," said
Virginia. "I'm sure your presence in the courtroom influenced the jury."

"Well, what else was it supposed to do? The lawyer,
Mr. Goldstein—"

"Goldberg," said Virginia.

"Goldberg, then. He wasn't our regular lawyer. He
insisted on my being in court."

"Did Sky insist on your being in court too?" said
Virginia.

"He asked me to be. It was Mr. Goldberg that did the
insisting."

"Lovey, if you don't mind my saying so, you've been
had," said Virginia.

"So it would appear," said Lovey. "Well, live and
learn, live and learn."

Virginia Vernon's exclusive story, which earned her
a bonus of $50, was on the street at seven o'clock that
evening. It was oversympathetic to Lovey and could not

fail to create the impression that she had made her
courtroom appearances as a final concession to Sky's
selfishness. Lovey, who not only had made no plans
to go away with Sky but had made no plans at all, was
having dinner in the apartment alone except for the
servants, when Sky telephoned. "Congratulations," he
said.

"On what?" said Lovey.

"On making such a shit-heel of me. You didn't lose
any time."

"I don't know what you're talking about."

"Your article in the *News*."

"My article in the *News*? You're drunk."

"I'm on the way, but I can still read. Exclusive, copyright. Who the hell is Virginia Vernon? All right, baby.
If that's how you want to play, that's how we'll play. I
wanted to—I was hoping we could straighten this out
between ourselves, but not after this article of yours."

"I haven't seen it, and it isn't my article."

"Don't be a liar on top of everything else. You knew
fucking well I'm sterile and I couldn't have been the
father of that kid. You knew that dame's a whore. It
didn't cost you so much to sit there in court. But little
did I know that you were sore because I screwed a few

dames. Little did I know that you were just waiting to get your revenge in print. All right, Lovey, you're getting your revenge. But bear this in mind, baby. You're not going to get a cent out of me. You can go to Reno or any damn place you please, but if you try to get any alimony or anything else, I'll contest your divorce and I'll make you look like the easiest pushover in town."

"Do your worst," said Lovey.

"Don't worry, I will. All the time we were married I never said a word about your mother, locked up in the loony-bin. But that article of yours! I never begrudged you a nickel, not a cent, even when I knew you were in the hay with that muff-diver saxophone player."

"Sky, why don't *you* go to Reno and divorce *me?* Or are you too much of a gentleman to do that? I'll leave here tomorrow and go back to Philadelphia."

"Got you scared, have I?"

"Yes, you have. Not about myself, but about my mother. But if I ever see one word about her in the newspapers, I'll kill you. Now just remember that, Sky. Say what you please about me, but keep her out of it."

"Do you want me to keep Marcy Bancroft out of it too?" said Sky.

"Marcy Bancroft? The girl I went to school with?"

"You want to talk to her? She's right here with me," said Sky.

"Yes, I'll talk to her," said Lovey. "Put her on."

"Hello, Lovey," said Marcy Bancroft. "You remember me? The firebug?"

"Hello, Marcy," said Lovey. "It's been ages. What are you doing with Sky?"

"The same thing he's doing with me," said Marcy.

"I mean, when did you meet him? How did you get to know him?"

"How did I get to know him? Why, I was recommended to him by a friend of his."

"When was that?"

"When was it? The day before yesterday, I guess it was."

"Where have you been living all this time?"

"A little small talk, Lovey? Why don't you ask me to have lunch with you and I'll tell you all about it."

"Maybe sometime, but not now."

"Oh, not now, eh, Lovey?"

"Marcy, are you in bed with Sky?"

"Why? Would you care to join us? . . . Sky says no, so I withdraw the invitation. How's your mother?"

"Not very well. She's in an institution."

"I know how that is, I was in an institution myself. And your mother didn't do a thing to help me, although she should have."

"Maybe she should have, maybe not," said Lovey. "I know what you're talking about, Marcy. And you shouldn't talk about it. Hardly anybody knows that you were one of my poor mother's girl friends, but they will if you blab it to people like Schuyler Childs. If you were thinking of being the next Mrs. Schuyler Childs, you'd better give up that idea."

"Who said I had any such idea?" said Marcy.

"I did. It's obvious, or you wouldn't be where you are now. And believe me, I don't care. But don't fool yourself, Marcy. Underneath the playboy, Sky is the most conservative, snobbish man I've ever known. You haven't a prayer."

"He married you," said Marcy.

"Oh, but he knew that my father was F. Willingham Lewis, of Philadelphia. That was one of the first things he asked me, the night we eloped. Those things mean a lot to Sky. In fact, they're the only things that do mean anything, and that's why he's so cross about the article in the paper. Are you listening, Sky?"

"Yes, I'm listening," said Sky.

"I was sure you would be. Now you two be happy together," said Lovey, and hung up.

Thus, almost with the suddenness that it began, ended the romantic team of Sky and Lovey, Lovey and Sky. But Lovey was always known as Lovey Childs, in or out of print; and Sky was all too often, for him, identified as the first husband of Lovey Childs.

Virginia Vernon, who had become the recognized authority on Lovey Childs, was trying to persuade her managing editor that the close contact with Lovey was potentially too valuable to neglect.

"I agree with you," said Howard Pierce. "Take her to lunch, the best damn place in town. We'd rather spend twenty or thirty bucks on Lovey Childs than give it to some police lieutenant in The Bronx."

"I wasn't exactly thinking of lunch, Howard."

"No?"

"I was thinking that if you put me on special assignment I could go to Reno when she does."

"What's in that for us?"

"A series of articles on what a society dame does while she's taking the cure. It could be sensational, Howard."

"We did a series about Reno two or three years ago."

"I remember it, and it stank," said Virginia Vernon.

"Yes, it stank all right," said Pierce. "We paid a guy fifteen hundred bucks and expenses, and all we got out of it was a strong hint that maybe some of those dames were bedding down with cowboys."

"That was the trouble. You got a guy from Los Angeles—"

"Eddie Parmenteer."

"Eddie Parmenteer," said Virginia Vernon.

"Eddie gave us a lot of good stuff during the Arbuckle case, but the Reno stuff, I was ashamed to run it. I called him up long distance and I said to him to stop writing for the *Christian Science Monitor*. Jesus, in the Arbuckle case Eddie was the first guy to tell us about the icicle in the girl's twat. I was always sorry we couldn't run it the way Eddie wrote it, but at the last minute we had to rewrite it. Orders from upstairs. Then every paper in the country had it a couple days later, but we had it first. No, Ginny, I don't go for another Reno series."

"Okay, Howard. But remember I came to you first," said Virginia Vernon.

"What do you mean by that?"

"I had an offer from a magazine—"

"What magazine?"

"I can't tell you," she said.

"What'll they pay you?"

"Seven-fifty apiece for four articles, plus all expenses," she said.

"Three thousand bucks, plus whatever you swindle them."

"Plus a job on the staff," she said.

"Oh, come on, Ginny, you wouldn't leave *us*. You couldn't."

"For that kind of money I'd have to. And I'm getting tired of dragging my fanny after every cloak-and-suiter's girl friend, having them slam the door in my face."

"You'd be back here inside of a month, Ginny. I wouldn't work on a magazine for twice the dough I'm getting."

"You wouldn't, but I would," she said.

"Let me think about it."

"All right. One, two, three, four, five, six—when I get up to fifty."

"This isn't a bluff, is it?" said Pierce.

"Seven, eight, nine, ten, eleven," she said.

"Ah, shut up. I think it is a bluff."

"Then call it," said Ginny.

"Oh, I know you could always go to the *Mirror*," he said.

"You bet I could," said Ginny.

"The magazine I wouldn't mind, but if you went over to the *Mirror*—all right, you win, you cunt."

"From you I consider that a term of endearment. It makes up for all those years you never made a pass at me."

"I always understood you were strictly sidesaddle," he said.

"Never take anything for granted, Howie. You'll never get anywhere in the newspaper business that way."

"What I'd like to do right now is give you a punch in the nose," he said. He put on his black-rimmed glasses and wrote on a notepad: "Vernon—special assignment." He removed the glasses. "But no society dames sleeping with cowboys, unless you give us names, dates, places, damp towels, old cundrums."

"Howie, did you really go to Harvard? It says so in *Who's Who*."

"Yes, I was there a couple of years. Old Man Hearst went to Harvard too, you know."

"And Phillips Exeter, you went there too?"

"Yes. I was at Exeter and Harvard with Robert Benchley. Why? Aren't I your idea of the Harvard type?"

"You're not even my idea of a man that says 'aren't I?' "

"If you had grown up in a Congregationalist parsonage, you'd want to forget it too."

"What's so different about a Congregationalist parsonage? I grew up in a Presbyterian one."

"Well, I'll be a son of a bitch. I never knew that. I always thought your mother was a madam in Port Said."

"That was Mother. Papa was the religious one," she said.

"Get out of here, I have work to do," he said. "Oh, one last question."

"Was I bluffing? You'll never, never, never know," said Virginia Vernon.

The Childs family had persuaded Sky to let Lovey get the divorce. His mother, his uncle, and his sister, and the family lawyer employed separate arguments, but they were united in the opinion that there had been quite enough notoriety for a while. The dowager Mrs. Childs had been in seclusion in Scotland during the paternity trial, and she wanted to come home to New Jersey. Uncle Peter Childs was concerned about his election to a trusteeship at Princeton. Sister Millicent Childs Rembrandt had a daughter almost ready to go away to Miss Brandon's School, and a messy divorce at this time would surely keep the girl out. Adrian Rembrandt, Millicent's husband, was known among his friends as a tower of Jello, but even he spoke to Sky to induce him to stay out of print. "All right, Adrian," said Sky. "But one of these days the cops are going to swoop down on you and your pansy boy friends, and then we'll really see some notoriety."

"I haven't the *faintest* idea what you *mean*," said Adrian Rembrandt.

"Oh, you thilly boy, you have tho. You and thothe dragth you go to in Harlem," said Sky.

"Millicent knows all about that," said Adrian.

"I'm sure she does. But I wasn't thinking of Millicent. I was thinking of the cops."

"They're private costume parties, by invitation only," said Adrian. "Not just anybody and everybody can come."

"Well, the first I ever heard about them was from a taxi driver, that's how private they are," said Sky. "A *colored* taxi driver."

"I know. We're not having them in Harlem any more," said Adrian. "We have them in somebody's house."

"Did you ever get a prize, Adrian?"

"Second. I was cheated out of first prize. The boy that got first prize—not that he wasn't simply gorgeous —but he was wearing a gown that one of the jury designed, and that's against all the rules. It was decidedly unfair. Imagine what chance anyone else had when one of the jury had his own dress in the contest. The worst *kind* of cheating."

"Yeah, well life is full of those disappointments," said Sky.

"You're a bitch, Schuyler. I never know when you're in earnest."

"I've never been in earnest. But—"

"I know. If you're ever in earnest, he'll know. I know that old gag. But meanwhile, Schuyler, not as a favor to me, but for Millicent and your mother, take it easy in that divorce. Go abroad for a while, away from these horrid tabloids."

"Adrian, are you the father of Millicent's kid?"

"Well, I could be, you know. She doesn't look very much like me, but she has the same coloring. Millicent and I used to copulate a lot in those days. We still do, but not as much. If we don't see too much of each other, it comes back to us. But she's like all of you Childses—possessive. She wants me to give up all my friends, and I just won't do it. I'd die without my friends, I'd just curl up and die. Millicent doesn't care that much about friends. Outside of her family she—well, a man to sleep with, but they never get to be friends of hers. If I'm not the father of our daughter, I know who is, and Millicent can't stand him. But every once in a while I can tell when she's been sleeping with him again. She gets all glowing and purring and nice to everybody for a few days. Then he has to go back to where he lives, back to his wife, and Millicent cries and cries because he's so mean to her. But the funny part of it is, she'd much rather be married to me. He's really a nobody with a big tool, and she wouldn't put up with him for six months. Or he with her, I might add. They've been sleeping together for fifteen years and in all that time he never asked her to marry him. He's no fool. Imagine Millicent in Chicago, married to not quite top drawer, and trying to lord it over those Chicago women? They'd cut her into little pieces, like sausage. Oh, I may not be such a much, but we were Hudson River patroons before you Childses had a pot to piddle in, and Millicent knows it and your mother knows it. *My* mother thought you Childses were rather common—and I *still* think so. You, especially, Sky. You're instinctively common, wanting to get your revenge on Lovey by smearing her all over the papers."

"Oh, balls, I'm not going to do that. I said I wasn't, and I'm not," said Sky.

"You'd better not," said Adrian. "I like Lovey. She was always very kind to me, and I'd be on her side."

Sky went abroad, to Paris and the south of France, to the Swiss Alps, to a chamois shoot in a schloss, to places carefully chosen for the entertainments they offered and for another reason: his preferences were for places where the English were few in number and small in influence, where he was not likely to encounter friends or relatives of the late Captain the Honourable T. A. B. Flaxham. Certain pals of Tommy Flaxham's had never accepted the official exoneration of Sky Childs; on one occasion, a luncheon at a Long Island golf club, two Englishmen and their wives rose and pointedly departed as Sky and Lovey were being seated at the next table.

Sky went abroad, and Lovey went to Reno. She had reservations at a ranch a few miles from the town, and she had been there less than a week when Virginia Vernon rode up on an ugly piebald cow pony. "Hello, Virginia," said Lovey. "There's no getting away from you, is there?"

"I hope you don't mind," said Virginia. "I'm here to do a series of articles for my paper. On Reno, not on you."

"Can I count on that? If you're writing about me,

I don't want to talk to you. You're why I'm here, you know."

"So I heard, but I couldn't believe Sky would be so silly," said Virginia.

"Then you don't know Sky—and you ought to," said Lovey. "I *could* have you ejected from here."

"Don't do that, Lovey. I have to make a living, you know. And anyway you'll be gone, a free woman, by the time the series starts running."

"Yes, but who knows? I may want to come back here some other time," said Lovey. "All right, come on in."

She saw Virginia nearly every day. They would ride a few miles together—Virginia was more at ease than Lovey in a stock saddle, and did not mind at all sitting to the trot. "My father was a preacher, and we lived in Iowa, Nebraska, and South Dakota. I learned to ride bareback," she said. She had been to two high schools and two state universities. Her father never lasted very long in a parish, and most of the time there was not a dollar in the house. "As a matter of actual fact, I was richer in college than I'd ever been in my life before. I took jobs in stores, working behind the counter. And I used to make some money doing the girls' laundry, the nicer underwear. I used to get twenty-five cents for pressing a girl's dress. Even now I still press my own. I never went home for Christmas. The department stores paid me as much as twenty dollars a week, eight o'clock in the morning to ten at night. I also did a certain amount of shoplifting. It was like taking candy from a baby during the Christmas rush. I had an accomplice, a girl in my class who had a Christmas job in a drug store. I'd let her steal stockings and underwear, and she'd let me steal anything I could lay my hands on—perfume, rolls of film, fountain pens. She and I ate our lunch at the soda fountain and never paid a check. The soda jerk wasn't interested in me, but every chance he got he was feeling her behind. Never did anything else, just liked to feel her behind. I've never been able to understand that about men. What do they get out of it?"

"I think that's all some of them can do, but it makes them seem manly," said Lovey.

"Very likely," said Ginny. "She would have gone to bed with him, but all he wanted to do was get her a little excited, and leave her that way. I *hate* that."

"Yes," said Lovey.

"This place is full of frustrated women. I had no idea. You can see it in all their faces. Of course a lot of them are afraid they're being spied on, and I suppose some of them are. Especially the ones that do go to bed with the cowboys."

"You hear about that, but I don't know any," said Lovey.

"Would you sleep with a cowboy?"

"Not with any I've seen," said Lovey.

"No, I mean seriously," said Ginny.

"How can I say? I married Sky the first night I met him," said Lovey.

"Yes, I understand that all right. But would you go to bed with a man for nothing but sex?"

"I might, I guess," said Lovey. "That's really what it was with Sky, at first. I didn't know a thing about him the first time I met him. Then we did fall in love with each other, for a while."

They were back at Lovey's cabin, a comfortable enough shack with a sitting-room, bedroom, kitchen and bath. "Can I stay and talk?" said Ginny.

"As long as you don't mind talking while I have a tub. I like a hot bath after a ride. Help yourself. There's some gin in the kitchen." Lovey ran a tub and undressed. "You O.K.?" she said.

Ginny was in the sitting-room. She held up a shot glass, half filled with gin. "Perfectly content," she said.

"I'll be out of here in five minutes," said Lovey, and lowered herself into the hot water that came up to her chin. She could hear Ginny moving about, but the bath was so luxurious that she made no effort to keep track of time. She was conscious, but still and silent.

"I decided to join you," said Ginny, and the effect of the sound of her voice was as startling as Ginny herself, standing naked in the doorway. She had the shot glass in her hand and was unselfconscious of her nudity. She was thin, with firm breasts that were hardly fuller than a boy's, and an extraordinary mat of pubic hair.

"You'll have to wait for more hot water," said Lovey. "It takes a while."

"Don't bother. I'll just take a quick dip," said Ginny. She lowered her hand to test the water's warmth. "Still warm as toast," she said, and gently rubbed Lovey's shoulders. She put the shot glass on top of the laundry hamper, knelt beside the tub and with the other hand rubbed Lovey's breasts.

"I'd rather you didn't do that, Ginny," said Lovey.

"Just a little? I can see you like it," said Ginny.

"I don't really like it," said Lovey.

"But I do. So pretty."

"I think you had too much gin," said Lovey.

"Not too much. Just enough."

Lovey leaned forward and took the stopper out of the tub. "Be sensible, Ginny. Put your clothes on and go home." Lovey stood up.

"I couldn't, now," said Ginny. "We have to go through with it."

"With what? We don't have to go through with anything."

"You don't know me. I want you too much. Please, Lovey, please be nice. It isn't much to ask, when I want you so much. You won't have to do anything."

"Ginny, please get out of the way."

"I warn you, I won't be responsible. Please don't make me do something awful," said Ginny. "I *know* myself."

Lovey hesitated. She put a skimpy bath towel over her bosom.

"Let me dry you," said Ginny. "I'll dry you and you won't catch cold."

"I can dry myself, thank you."

"No, let me. I'll dry you and you'll be nice and dry and relaxed."

"This is ridiculous."

"Just let me dry you. Just stand there and when I

finish drying you I'll go home. Will you let me do that? I won't be rough. I'll be very gentle." Ginny took the towel out of Lovey's hands and rubbed her shoulders and arms with it, lightly fluffing the towel so that in her touch Ginny made the harsh texture soft and delicate. She took longer than necessary and put off drying between Lovey's legs to the very last.

"I'll do the rest," said Lovey, and Ginny handed her the towel.

"Do you see how gentle I was?" said Ginny. "Wasn't I gentle?"

"Yes," said Lovey.

"I've calmed down now," said Ginny.

"That's good," said Lovey. She put on a kimono. "Now why don't you get dressed? It's getting dark, and you have your horse to put away."

"Couldn't I spend the night here?"

"No, Ginny. I'm very tired and relaxed and I want you to go."

"I can't. I can't leave you. How can you be so cruel? I won't hurt you."

"I'm getting impatient, Ginny. What do you want to do?"

"You know what I want to do," said Ginny.

"You want me to lie down and let you kiss me. Is that what you want?"

"Terribly."

"If I do, is that all?"

"I swear it is, and nobody will ever know," said Ginny.

Lovey lay on the bed and opened the kimono, submissively. But Ginny shook her head. "Close your eyes," she said.

"Why?"

"I won't have any pleasure if you don't have any pleasure. I can give you pleasure if you'll let me."

Lovey closed her eyes, and for a long time the sensation was that of Ginny's fingertips in an innocent caress from the soles of her feet to the back of her neck, the fingers darting from place to place in a series of pleasant surprises until Lovey took her breast in her hand and held it in an invitation to be kissed. Then she realized that the slow easy caresses had accomplished their purpose and she was ready for all the pleasure that Ginny could create. It ceased to matter whether she was producing the sensation or Ginny was producing it for her, but at last it came as an unendurable novelty. Ginny looked up at her with a proud smile, and nothing was said.

Ginny handed her a lighted cigarette and lay down beside her. "I almost fainted," said Lovey.

Ginny nodded, still smiling. "I didn't want to ask you before," said Ginny. "With a man, but never with a girl?"

"Never with a girl. Not that much with a man. With a man, but not that completely."

"How would a man know?" said Ginny.

"I guess that's it," said Lovey. "You're so *proud* of yourself, Ginny."

"I know I am."

"Did anything happen to you?"

"Oh, yes."

"It's a terrible thing, but I can't do it to you."

"You mean you don't want to. You're a selfish little pig, aren't you?" said Ginny.

"I have to tell you the truth," said Lovey.

"No. You could have done it to me, without saying anything. But no, you had to tell me you didn't want to."

"I don't really think you want me to," said Lovey.

"You convinced yourself of that. You're a selfish little pig, all take and no give."

"I can't help it, Ginny. I could make myself do it, but you'd know I didn't want to."

"Try it and see," said Ginny.

"I may want to sometime, but not now," said Lovey.

"Oh, you'll want to sometime, I know that. But it'll be someone else, not me."

"Is that the way it is?"

"That's usually the way."

"Then I'm one of you now, is that it?"

"You bet you are," said Ginny.

"I know I am. My mother is one of you. My own mother," said Lovey.

"Well, what if she is?"

"What if she is? She's in the booby hatch, that's what if she is. And I don't want to end up in the booby hatch."

"Christ, we're all in some kind of a booby hatch. What do you think Reno is? My mother spent her whole life in a booby hatch, only they called it a parsonage. My father escaped from the booby hatch by tying a rope around his neck. That husband of yours—Christ, if he isn't ready for the booby hatch! I was in the booby hatch for you because I thought you'd make a nice piece of trade, and now I'm in another booby hatch because you won't go down on me. Well, I finally made you, Lovey. That's really why I came to Reno, because I was on the make for you."

"I hope it was worth it," said Lovey.

"Sweetie, it was. And it was worth waiting for. I got hot pants for you when I covered your elopement, but you were always cock-struck. Now you don't have to be cock-struck any more. You can give us girls a chance at that nice pussy of yours. And you will, if the cowboys don't get there first. Only they didn't. *I* got there first."

"Ginny, did you drink that whole bottle of gin?"

"Well, you kept me waiting quite a while. And it wasn't a whole bottle. A little more than half. But I'd have made a pass at you without the gin. One always knows when the opportune moment has come, and today was it."

"You're in no condition to ride that horse back to your ranch. I'll have them put him up for the night."

"And what about me? Do I sleep in the stable?"

"Stop feeling sorry for yourself. You can stay here," said Lovey.

"Can you get another bottle of gin?" said Ginny. "I'll pay for it."

"If you'll put some clothes on," said Lovey. She went to the telephone, which was on a table beside the bed, and while she was giving the order Ginny sat close to her and fondled her breasts.

"I'm crazy about you, I really am," said Ginny. "Are they bringing the gin?"

"Right away," said Lovey.

"I'm absolutely crazy about you," said Ginny.

"Put on my bathrobe. The waiter'll be here any minute," said Lovey. "He can lead the horses back to the barn."

"You drink some gin and catch up with me," said Ginny.

"I never drink gin. It makes me sick."

"Then why did you have it here?" said Ginny.

"I don't know. The bathrobe."

Ginny stood up and unsteadily got the bathrobe and put it on. "You could get some whiskey."

"I don't want any whiskey," said Lovey.

"It is getting dark. They just put the lights on," said Ginny.

"Anybody could see in," said Lovey. She went about and lowered the Venetian blinds. "Be nice if someone was watching a few minutes ago."

"I wish they'd hurry with the gin," said Ginny. "I go for weeks without a drink and never miss it, but when I drink I like to drink. I never had a drink till I went to work in New York. I only drink for the effect."

"Doesn't everybody?" said Lovey.

"But sometimes I go for weeks without a single drop. Some people can't get through the day without it."

There was knocking on the sitting-room door. Lovey took a five-dollar bill from her purse and went to the door.

The waiter, an undersized man in a white jacket too big for him, handed her the bottle in a paper sack. "Be three dollars, Mrs. Childs."

"Thank you, and keep the change. Could you take the horses to the stable? My friend turned her ankle."

"Be right pleased to, ma'am. I hope the ankle ain't hurt bad," said the waiter.

"It's nothing serious. Hot compresses should do the trick," said Lovey.

The man mounted Lovey's horse and led the other away, and Lovey closed the door. She handed the bottle to Ginny, who quickly unscrewed the cap and took a swig.

"Sure you don't want some?" said Ginny.

"No thanks," said Lovey.

"A turned ankle. That was quick thinking," said Ginny. "It explains just about everything, in case he had an evil mind. Well, I feel better. How do you feel?"

"Perfectly well," said Lovey.

"Shut out the world, sweetie," said Ginny. "It's just you and I. Who's going to know the difference?"

"You and I are," said Lovey.

"The whole thing's a booby hatch, anyway," said Ginny. She took another swig of gin. "I know you're trying to get me tight so I'll pass out. But I'm no good to you if I pass out. Be truthful, don't you want me to make love to you again?"

"Yes and no."

"The yes part is the truthful part. You're nervous because I will and nervous because I won't. I'm the same way. I'm even more excited than the first time. I tell you, I'm crazy about you. But this time you're a little crazy about me. I did something wonderful for you, and you want to do something wonderful for me. Is that right?"

"I guess so," said Lovey.

Ginny dropped her bathrobe and removed Lovey's kimono, and they stood close together in an embrace. "Isn't it exciting?" said Ginny.

"Yes."

"Are you going to be nice to me?" said Ginny.

"Yes."

"As nice as I was to you?" said Ginny.

"Yes."

"That's the way you'll find out how nice it is," said Ginny. She lay on the bed and Lovey made love to her exactly as she remembered Ginny's having made love to her.

"Was that right?" said Lovey.

"Oh, couldn't you tell! Couldn't you tell! You know it was."

"And now I really am one of you," said Lovey.

"No. You never will be."

"But you said it was right," said Lovey.

"Oh, I love you, terribly and forever. But you could go with a man, this minute, and I couldn't. You were perfect for me, and I'll never be perfect for you. For me, this is everything. For you, not quite."

"I want to be one of you," said Lovey.

"Till you get over Sky Childs."

"But I liked this and I didn't think I would," said Lovey.

"You're a woman, a woman likes to please," said Ginny. "I want to please you. Shall I?"

"Yes," said Lovey.

But this time was not as good. It was good, as a calmly prolonged experience in sensuality, but one that need not have come to a climax, could as well have ended in sleep and, in fact, did. When she opened her eyes Ginny was sitting up beside her, making endless figures on Lovey's breasts and belly with the tips of her fingers. "I had a nap," said Lovey.

"A long one," said Ginny.

"Oh, really? How long?"

"Oh—close to a half an hour," said Ginny. "You had a bad dream, or a nightmare."

"I have a lot of them. Who was it this time?"

"You don't speak very distinctly in your sleep. Marcia? Would that be one of the names?"

"Close. Close enough."

"And your mother. If you call her Mummy."

"Yes, they're the usual ones," said Lovey. "And Sky."

"Didn't mention Sky."

"I didn't dream about you, but I did dream about your father. I guess it was your father. Hanging himself. Only it didn't stay your father. It turned into my father, and *he* didn't hang himself. Still he did break his neck. I'd hate to try to make any sense out of my dreams. What's his name—Freud himself couldn't make any sense out of them. You're awake, and you were supposed to be the one that would pass out." She put her arms around Ginny's waist and gently kissed her small breast.

"You poor kid," said Ginny, and they wept.

The house where Dorothy Lewis was living out her
life was high in the mountains above the Lebanon Valley.
It was called The Gables, and the name, so nearly anony-
mous, told something of the character of the place. From
the main highway in the valley a visitor turned off into a
township road and then began looking for a sign that
was big enough for those who might be looking for it,
but easily missed by anyone else. At this sign the visitor
turned into a private driveway, a dirt road that was kept
uninvitingly in bad repair. At the end of the road stood
The Gables, originally the country home of a Reading

brewer who had memories of Austria. The house could accommodate eight inmates, and they were there on a permanent basis. No one but a woodsman with an ax was likely to penetrate the surrounding forest, thick as it was and known to be infested with copperheads and rattlers. Most of the windows were barred, and a German shepherd dog had the run of the place. The owner of The Gables was an osteopath, Dr. Frank Foltz by name, a man of probity who loved the woods and had discovered a profitable way to combine business with pleasure. His wife shared his fondness for the wild life. They would have been happier without the paying inmates, but they could not have maintained such an ideal establishment on Frank Foltz's income as a practising osteopath in the city of Reading. Essie Foltz was a trained nurse, a graduate of the Reading Hospital, very good at finding the nerve when administering hypodermics, a soothingly attentive listener to the prattling of the inmates. The cooking was done by Essie's widowed sister, and the rest of the staff consisted of a powerfully built orderly and two middle-aged Lebanon Valley women who went home at night. All the inmates were women between the ages of forty-five and eighty, and such was the reputation of The Gables that it always had a waiting list. There was not much to do for the inmates except to feed them and try to keep them clean. They all needed dental care, and none of them got it.

It was always a shattering experience for Lovey to visit her mother. On the first visit Dorothy wept uninterruptedly, offering no explanation, answering no questions. On the second visit Mrs. Foltz said that Dorothy was much better, and Lovey was able to have an intelligent conversation with her until the very end, when Dorothy, rising to accompany Lovey to the front door, said, "If you ever happen to run into my daughter, please tell her that we'll be down to see her very soon." On the third visit the Foltzes would not let Lovey see her mother. She was under sedation, they said, and the doctor from Reading had forbidden any visitors. On the fourth visit Dorothy's breath was so bad that Lovey had to keep away from her, but Dorothy talked incessantly about her plans for a fancy dress party she was giving at the Bellevue-Stratford. "We've invited the Prince of Wales and that Long Island crowd. I'm going as Dolley Madison. She was my cousin, you know. He loves to dance, although I may be a bit tall for him. Of course with those low heels I won't be quite so tall." On the fifth visit she told Lovey a fantastic story about a night in Germany when she was on her honeymoon with Billy Lewis and Billy brought a woman in to make love to her. The woman became very angry because Billy did not give her enough money, and she set fire to the hotel. On the sixth visit Dorothy asked Lovey to mail a secret letter she had written to President Wilson, in which she accused Joe Fuller of stealing a million dollars from Billy Lewis. "I can't mail it here because Joe has had me locked up," said Dorothy. "He's afraid of what I'll tell."

On this visit Mrs. Foltz said, "Now I don't know where she ever got her information from, but she heard you got a divorce in Reno, Nevada. We try our best to keep such information away from our patients, but one person will get a hold of a newspaper and no telling who gets their hands on it. I told her you'd be coming to see her and she said your husband took all your money away from you."

"Well, of course that's not true," said Lovey.

"I know, I didn't see anything about that in the papers," said Mrs. Foltz.

"Mrs. Foltz, isn't there ever *any* sign of improvement?" said Lovey. "I know they've given up on her, but you see her oftener than most people. Don't you ever see anything that could give us, her, any hope?"

"Well, there are some days she's better than other days. That's when I can see what she was like before she took sick. But the good days are few and far between. They have an operation they perform, but so far I understand they don't have much success with it, only temporary. If she was one of mine, my mother or like that, I'd sooner not have the operation. Why put them through all that if there's no guarantee they'll get better? And some of them I'm told get worse. If she was mine I'd much rather leave her the way she is. She has a good appetite most of the time, and you know they can just sit there, you don't know what's going on in their mind, but they can sit there for hours at a time and they seem content. But then something will set them off, and you wouldn't want her *with* people. They have to be watched. Sometimes they fight amongst themselves. Just be sitting there as quiet as a mouse, not even talking to one another. Then all of a sudden the one of them'll go at the other tooth and nail. *Tooth and nail,* I don't exaggerate. Scratching, biting, and you know some of them still have a lot of strength left. You'd be surprised how strong some of them are. That's why I say you can't leave them alone for a minute. There always has to be somebody near to separate them, and you never know what sets them off. It's like as if they were some kind of an animal. You know how one dog'll turn on another. It's what they call a sixth sense that tells them that the other is thinking up something."

"And my mother does that?"

"Yes, your mother does that. The most polite and refined ones are just the same as anybody else."

"Well—will you let me see her now?" said Lovey.

"I'm going to let you look at her, to see she's in good health and getting enough to eat and all. But I'd rather you didn't talk to her. We have her in what we call sem-eye-isolation."

"Does that mean locked up?"

"We're keeping her away from the others. She was all right when we told her you were coming, but five minutes later she said someone was coming here to take her money, and not to let them in. You'll be able to have a good look at her through a slot in the door. I'd have called you up, but you were on the way."

"I'm not afraid of her," said Lovey. "I'd like to go in and talk to her."

"Well, if you go in we'd want you to sign a paper that we warned you. Hereafter it'd be better if you brought Mr. Williams with you, your lawyer. It makes him sad when he comes to see her, but we'd rather you brought him. She's always glad to see him, but she gets him mixed up with somebody else."

"Yes, he told me that," said Lovey. "I hate to ask him to make the trip."

"Well, it doesn't have to be him, as long as it's somebody you can depend on. I'll type out the paper for you to sign. I know it by heart." Mrs. Foltz, a slow typist, wrote the release and gave it to Lovey. "Just sign there at the bottom," she said.

Lovey read the paper. It stated that the undersigned wished to visit the patient Dorothy Lewis unaccompanied by any member of the staff of The Gables, and assumed full responsibility for actions occurring during visit. Lovey signed, and Mrs. Foltz witnessed the signature.

"It's red tape, but we have to have it," said Essie Foltz. She put the paper in a folder and filed it away. "We can go have a look and then I'll let you in."

They went to Dorothy's room. "The door can't be locked from the inside. They think it can, but it can't. But you can see we can bolt it from the outside. Notice how narrow the slot is. But it's long, and you can see the whole inside of the room."

"Couldn't she hide in the closet?"

"It's locked," said Essie Foltz.

"Hasn't she got her own bathroom?"

"Yes, but the water's shut off in the tub. It's only on in the washstand and the toilet. The patients aren't allowed to take a bath without somebody there. The problem is to get some of them to take a bath at all. There, now you can have a look at her."

The slot was about an inch wide and a foot long. Dorothy was sitting on a chaise-longue, wearing a nightgown and a bathrobe that buttoned but did not have a cord. A book lay open in her lap. In a little while she began reading aloud, a passage from Willa Cather's novel *Death Comes for the Archbishop*. She read distinctly for two or three minutes, put the book down, stared straight ahead, and a minute or two later resumed reading aloud the same passage. She was like a child in a classroom, demonstrating her literacy but spiritually unmoved. She lay the book on her lap again and inspected her fingernails, holding her hands palm up then palm down, extending the hands one at a time. This went on for a considerable time and was followed by her inserting the tip of her little finger in her ear, shaking free a quantity of wax, studying the wax, and putting it in her mouth. Once again she resumed her reading of the passage from the Cather novel in the same monotonous fashion.

"Now do you want to go in?" said Essie Foltz.

"No," said Lovey. "I've seen enough."

Essie Foltz closed the slot. "It'd be a pity to get her all excited."

"How long has she had that book?"

"Since Sunday," said Essie Foltz. "She takes a new book out of the library every Sunday. She'll open it up and start reading out loud. If she loses her page she opens it up somewhere else. It seems to give her some comfort to read out loud to herself. But she's not always as peaceful as that, Mrs. Childs. That's why I'm glad you didn't go in. She likes to lie on the floor without any clothes on, and that's always a bad sign. That means she wants to have intercourse, and she gets very angry. I shouldn't say this, but sometimes I think it would be good for her if she *could* have intercourse. That's just my belief. You know, it's natural for a woman to want it, especially if she was married all that time. But never fear, Mark, the orderly, would never take advantage of her. He's the other way, if you know what I mean. Strong as an ox, but doesn't care for women. He does beautiful needlepoint and things like that. Nature plays funny tricks, that's for sure. Let's go back to the office and have a cup of coffee, or would you rather have tea? My sister baked a shoo-fly pie, and coffee goes better with it, but if you prefer tea we can have that."

Dr. Foltz came in while they were having their snack. "I was sorry I couldn't get here before, but we had a bank meeting," said Foltz. "Did you see your mother?"

"Through the slot," said Essie Foltz. "She was reading her book."

"Uh-huh. Well, that's what we call the calm before the storm," said Foltz. "How is Mrs. Minzer since I left?"

"Still asleep, the last I saw her," said Essie Foltz.

"The doctor's coming out from Reading before supper," said Foltz. "One of our patients, Mrs. Minzer. I want to have her moved to hospital. Organic trouble that we don't take care of. You know I'm not an M.D."

"Yes, I knew that," said Lovey.

"Sometimes I wish I'd gone on and got my M.D., but other times I'm just as glad I didn't. I see some of these M.D.'s, old before their time and not much to show for it. Well, how did your mother look to you? Physically, I mean."

"Very well, I guess. But I can't say I'm encouraged otherwise," said Lovey.

"No, I'm afraid not," said Foltz. "The air here is very good for her, and she has a good appetite. She could live to be a hundred."

"God, I hope not," said Lovey.

"I don't know, though. If we keep her healthy they may come along with some new discovery. Surgery. Drugs. Different things. She has a strong constitution. You see, the way I look at it, Mrs. Childs, we try to keep them as healthy as possible in case some new thing comes along like surgery, and they'll be ready for it. That's all we can do, give them the best of care as long as they're in our charge."

"But you know it's hopeless," said Lovey.

"When they're brought here that's the same as their own doctors saying it's hopeless, their own families. We keep them healthy, we see that they don't do away with themselves. We don't run the kind of an institution where they come for a cure."

"All hope abandon, ye who enter here," said Lovey.

"I never said any different," said Foltz. "And this is our eighteenth year."

"My goodness, so it is," said Essie Foltz. "That means Mrs. Minzer's been here close on to sixteen years. Her family spent a young fortune on her, when you think of it."

"It doesn't look as if she'll be here much longer," said Foltz. "We know what she has."

"Cancer," said Essie Foltz to Lovey.

Foltz nodded. "They won't know for sure till they operate, but that's what it is."

"Is that what's going to happen to my mother? Is that all she has to look forward to?" said Lovey.

"They don't look forward here, Mrs. Childs. The next meal is about as far ahead as they look," said Foltz.

Things were happening in and to the United States of America that Lovey Childs made no attempt to understand. A great many people were losing large and small sums of money—that was what it came down to. Financial disaster had always been a fact of life; in her own and her father's and her grandparents' generations there had always been spectacular instances of the rich becoming the poor. Not all the great houses in Chestnut Hill and on the Main Line were occupied by their original owners; one was not unfamiliar with the language of catastrophe. "They lost every cent . . . His grandfather used to own half of Philadelphia . . . Her mother was presented at Court . . . His uncle went to prison . . . Her father committed suicide on his private car . . . They never finished the house in Palm Beach . . . Her brother was lucky to get any job at all . . . That was the last they ever saw of Count Whatever-His-Name-Was . . . They had nothing, literally nothing." A few sons and daughters were sent off to New York and San Francisco and Cleveland and St. Louis to seek new fortunes by matrimony; a large number stayed in Philadelphia and waited among the only people they cared to know, biding their time until a husband or a wife died and patience was rewarded. Philadelphia money belonged in Philadelphia.

But the things that were happening in and to the United States were too frequent, too common, to be understood as Lovey had been able to understand the dramatic loss of a fortune by a friend of her father's and mother's. Thousands of people were losing money that they had never had, before they had had much chance to spend it. The bootblack in the Land Title building, who had lost $100,000 in the New York stock market, had never been anything but a bootblack who was the nominal owner of securities priced at $100,000. He could easily afford to lose $100,000 or a million. "Do you understand what I'm driving at?" said Grafton Williams.

"I guess so. I'm not sure," said Lovey.

"Most of the people you hear about as losing money in the stock market didn't even lose it in the stock market. Tony Bianco took a thousand dollars out of a little Italian bank in South Philadelphia, his life savings. He went to a broker's office, the branch of a New York firm, and said he wanted to buy some stock. 'What stock?' said the broker. I happen to know this whole story. Tony wasn't sure what stock. He wasn't even sure of the difference between stocks and bonds. But he found out soon enough. It wasn't long before Tony was offering *me* tips on the market, and my shoes weren't getting as good a shine as they used to. Also, he became a talkative bore."

"What do you mean he didn't lose it in the stock market?" said Lovey.

"He lost it on his knees, boring his customers. When he began to make money he should have given up being a bootblack and paid attention to his stocks. When the market began to collapse he was off shining shoes, and his brokers had to sell him out. No margin. It served him right, poor slob. But he didn't have enough respect for a hundred thousand dollars. In the nature of things, a bootblack must have respect for a hundred thousand dollars or he deserves to lose it. There, in a nutshell, is

what's been going on in this country. I'd like to think
we've learned a lesson, but I know we haven't. Now
then, what have you decided to do with yourself?"

"I want to get married and have children," said
Lovey.

"A worthy ambition, especially after what we've just
been talking about," said Grafton Williams. "Who is the
lucky man?"

"I haven't the faintest idea," said Lovey.

"In other words, you know what you want to do but
not who with," said Grafton Williams. "Are you going to
go on living in Philadelphia?"

"What if I sold the house and took an apartment?"

"Oh, dear. Houses are going begging these days,
Lovey," said Grafton Williams. "The Catholics are going
to pay a lot less for the property than they would have
before. They're our only hope now. As long as you were
married to Schuyler Childs, you had nothing to worry
about. But you took nothing from him—an expensive
gesture on your part."

"What have I got left?"

"With the stock market the way it is, I'd say less than
ten thousand a year. As long as your mother's still alive,
you can't touch that trust fund. When she dies it all goes

to you, but meanwhile it represents no income for you."

"Why, I'm a pauper," said Lovey. "I've never really thought about money."

"That's it, you've never had to, and under ordinary conditions you never would have. But there's been a combination of circumstances that couldn't have been much worse for you. Your father's estate, your mother's collapse, your divorce, and the stock market crash. Everybody is sure the market will come back, and it will. But nobody's saying when. I myself am not very optimistic. I don't go so far as to say it'll be a lot worse before it's better. But I think real recovery is a long way off. This isn't just a stock market phenomenon. It's deep in the national economy, the world economy. Over-expansion. Loose credit. Inflated values as a result of stock market speculation. It may be ten years before we see real recovery, and God only knows what can happen during those years. You picked a wrong time to get rid of a rich husband, but at least there's always a market for an attractive young woman."

"Shall I become a prostitute?" said Lovey.

"If you set your price high enough. I'm told the competition is already quite fierce among the lower-priced ones. The going rate is twenty-five cents in some sections of Philadelphia. A police captain told me that there are young colored girls, children, that won't refuse a dime. After all, that's a loaf of bread. A loaf of bread and a bottle of ketchup are all that they put on the table, and the ketchup lasts a week. I'm glad I don't have to collect the rent in that part of Philadelphia."

"I suppose I ought to be thankful, but I'm not," said Lovey. "I'm just darn good and mad at Sky."

"Well, I've always had a low opinion of men that didn't work for a living."

"Daddy didn't work for a living," said Lovey.

"I never said I had a very high opinion of him, either," said Grafton Williams.

"Well, if you're going to criticize Daddy, you have a son that's just as much of a bum as either Daddy or Sky."

"He is indeed. He's home now, honoring us with his presence."

"Well, he's a man. Men can always do what they want to do," said Lovey. "Meanwhile, I suppose I ought to be looking for a job."

"It wouldn't be such a bad idea."

"Have you any suggestions?" said Lovey.

"None."

"Think what I have to offer. No education. A rather

messy divorce. A mother locked up in the crazy house. There must be something for somebody like me. I'm really the bottom of the barrel, aren't I?"

"Well, you can't do shorthand or typewriting, that's true. And even if you could, there are plenty of girls who could do it better and are looking for work. And yet something will come along. I can't believe that a young woman as attractive as you won't find something."

"What happens to people like me?" said Lovey. "Seriously, what happens? I can't say I'm broke, because I'm not. I'd be better off if I were, because then I'd be desperate and do something desperate. If I were homely and unattractive I could get a job scrubbing floors, but I'm not homely and unattractive and so I can't scrub floors. On the other hand, I'm attractive but dumb, and therefore you can't offer me a job as a receptionist, can you?"

"Have you ever taken a good look at our receptionist?"

"She's that Mrs. Turney, isn't she? She isn't exactly glamorous."

"No, but she's been with us thirty years, and she knows all our clients. If you'd promise to stay with us thirty years, I'd offer you her job, but you have a lot of living to do in the next thirty years—very little of it as a receptionist for a stodgy Philadelphia law firm. I have no idea what the future holds for you, Lovey, but it won't be with a stodgy law firm."

"I'm afraid you're right," said Lovey.

"What are you doing today, for instance?"

"I have a hair appointment at eleven, and I'm meeting Grace Wells for lunch, and Grace is going to the concert but I'm not. I'm taking the afternoon train for New York and going to a party there. It'll be my first New York party since Reno. I'll be at the St. Regis."

"So much for Mrs. Turney's job."

"You think I'm a wastrel, don't you?"

"A wastrel?" said Grafton Williams. "An odd word to use. I'm not even sure I know what it means."

"Neither am I—but it means a wastrel."

"Well, yes, I suppose you are," he said. "But you have a lot of time left. You're young, and who knows? You may meet someone at this party tonight, someone just the opposite of Sky Childs."

"Don't blame Sky for everything. He was as nice as he *could* be. But I wasn't much either. I was very shallow."

"I hate to interrupt this, but if you have a hair appointment at eleven, you'd better go," he said. "You're

not shallow, Lovey. You're just taking a long while growing up."

"And maybe I never will."

"Maybe you never will," he said.

The party that night was being given by an expatriate Philadelphia couple, who maintained an apartment in New York, lived there most of the time, but regarded themselves as Philadelphians and never closed their house in Chestnut Hill. Pauline Renzler Goodbody was in her thirties, known as Polly Good-enough-Body, and was the strikingly ugly wife of the handsome Archie Goodbody, who was known as Giggles. Giggles had had his nickname since before he was ten years old, and he was now forty. Lovey had seen a lot of the Goodbodys during her marriage to Sky, but the Goodbodys were thinking of dropping Sky, whom they had not invited to the party. "Of course he's liable to show up anyhow," said Polly. "We're having everybody."

Dinner was scheduled for eight o'clock, but at that hour Polly was still in her tub and Giggles was playing backgammon with Henry Gage, who had an apartment in the same building and would only take a minute to get into his Tuxedo. The first guests, a couple from Cedarhurst, arrived at eight-thirty, kibitzed the backgammon game until some more guests arrived and Giggles put on his Tuxedo jacket and acted as host. Miraculously all the guests were present at nine-thirty, and Polly Goodbody had them all seated by nine-forty-five. They were of all ages between twenty and sixty, and there were thirty-six of them.

Lovey, in a new dress by Hawes, went to the party alone. "Don't have anybody bring you," Polly had said. "I'm making sure we have plenty of extra men coming in later. In fact, that's the whole idea. It's your coming-out party, so to speak. There'll be dancing. I've invited a hundred people, and goodness knows how many Giggles has invited at the Racquet Club and Forty-two West Forty-nine. It's going to be a real rat-fuck. But private. And practically nobody from Philadelphia. What's the use of having Philadelphia people to this kind of party?" On Lovey's right at dinner was a Russian prince; known for his good looks and good manners and penury. He had a wife somewhere in France, who was making it difficult for him to marry a rich American—any rich American. On Lovey's left was her distant cousin Francis Lewis, three years out of Harvard, who was working for J. P. Morgan and all but engaged to a cousin on his mother's side, now hunting the tiger in India. "I gave you Alex because it never hurts a girl to have a good-looking man beside her. And I gave you Francis because a cousin is usually safe. I say *usually*, I don't say *always*." The small orchestra played non-dance music until the entree had been served, then at Polly's order they switched to fox trots, which they played without interruption until three A.M. Shortly after eleven o'clock the first of the people who had not been invited for dinner began to arrive, and they danced in the library and the hall, but inevitably they commingled with the dinner guests and the dinner party as such vanished and became a dance. Polly had planned it that way, even to the removal of the dinner tables, which made room for the dancers. "Nobody eats dessert any more," said Polly.

The Goodbodys' apartment, a duplex, was designed for parties, with the diningroom, kitchen, and library on the lower floor, and Polly's and Giggles' bedrooms on the floor above. There was no guest room. "We decided to discourage hanky-panky," said Polly. "Besides, it gives a girl an excuse for saying no. Anything a girl can't finish in the phone booth has to be done at home," and the phone booth under the stairs had a glass window in the door. "Of course there's always Henry Gage, two floors below, but then he'd have to know, and he talks." Henry Gage, divorced from his second wife, was Giggles Goodbody's best friend as well as his constant backgammon opponent, and Polly thoroughly disliked him. "I couldn't stand him when he was at St. Bartholomew's," said Polly. "And he hasn't gotten any better."

"Why do you live in the same building as Henry?" said Lovey.

"Unfortunately Henry was here first, and when we bought this apartment we actually had to have Henry's approval."

"He was best man at your wedding," said Lovey.

"An usher. Giggles' father was best man."

"I really don't think he's so bad," said Lovey.

"He reminds me too much of Grafton Williams. Apart from the fact that he isn't a lawyer, isn't a Philadelphian—"

"Apart from the fact that they both wear gold-rimmed glasses—"

"That's enough, isn't it?" said Polly. "It's all right for Grafton Williams to wear them, but not Henry Gage.

Divorced from two wives, and a real chaser. I never
knew why I disliked Henry so, but you've put your finger
right on it. He wears gold-rimmed spectacles and they're
wrong for him."

"Well, that's settled," said Lovey. They were chatting
in the bathroom, making small talk before the second part
of the party began in earnest.

"Just don't be fooled by those glasses. I know Henry
better than you do," said Polly. They went downstairs
together and the party was on.

Lovey had a good time. She knew everybody at the
party; some she had known all her life, and others she
had met during her marriage to Sky. There was no one
she had slept with, which was careful planning on the
part of her hostess, or ignorance, or both. In any case it
worked out very well. It became, in fact, a *nice* party,
and when the music stopped and it was time to go home
she found herself with Polly and Giggles and Henry
Gage. "I'll take you to your hotel," said Henry Gage.

"Oh, heavens, don't bother," said Lovey.

"No bother. It's still early," said Henry Gage.

"It's getting close to four o'clock," said Lovey.

"That's not late for you, unless you've changed."

"Maybe I have changed, but how would you know,
Henry? I've never been out with you."

"Well, while you two discuss it, I'm going to bed," said Polly. "Are you coming, Giggles?"

"I'll phone you in the morning," said Lovey.

"Not too early in the morning, please," said Polly. She was obviously annoyed with Henry Gage for hanging on. "Are you going to Sands Point tomorrow?"

"I wasn't asked," said Lovey.

"Yes you were. I heard Mary Ames ask you," said Polly.

"Oh, she was asking everybody," said Lovey.

"She didn't ask me," said Henry Gage.

"She may have made a point of not asking you, Henry," said Polly.

"Because I don't play croquet, no doubt," said Henry Gage.

"No, because she doesn't like you, is the more likely reason," said Polly.

"You two at it again," said Giggles. "Come on to bed, Polly."

"Goodnight, Polly," said Lovey. "It was a lovely party, it really couldn't have been nicer. Goodnight, Giggles. And thank you both."

In the elevator Henry Gage said, "I'm taking you to your hotel, unless you have any other ideas. How about the Clamhouse?"

"Harlem? No thanks, Henry. Just drop me at the St. Regis."

"Very well," said Henry, and when they got a taxi he told the driver, and then closed the glass divider. "I'm sorry Polly was so unpleasant. Do you know why?"

"I know she doesn't like you," said Lovey.

"That's what I asked you. Do you know why?"

"No," said Lovey.

"She thinks I'm a bad influence on Giggles."

"Well, are you?" said Lovey.

"Well, I suppose I am. Are you sure you don't want to go to Harlem?"

"Is that your bad influence? Taking Giggles to Harlem?"

"We've been there together, but Polly's been with us."

"Whose idea was Harlem?" said Lovey.

"Originally, I guess it was Giggles'. Giggles isn't the Mr. Purity you might think."

"I never thought he was. I never thought Polly was, either. Or you. Or me. Or any of us, for that matter."

"Why won't you come to Harlem with me?" said Henry Gage.

"You're not going to the Clamhouse, are you? You

must have some place more interesting than that," said Lovey.

"Well, I have, if you're interested."

"I might be, but not tonight, Henry," said Lovey. "I'm very tired. I got up at seven o'clock this morning, and besides we're in evening clothes. People ought not to go to Harlem in evening clothes."

"I agree with you there," said Henry. "Sometime when you're in New York we'll go, not in evening clothes."

"All right," said Lovey.

"That's a promise?"

"It's a promise," said Lovey.

He made the taxi wait while he saw her inside the hotel, and that was the last she ever saw of Henry Gage. Apparently he had the taxi drive him to Harlem, paid off the driver, and presumably went to a joint. His body, fully clothed, was found the next afternoon on the banks of the Harlem River above 150th Street. The throat was cut and the skull was fractured, leading to the belief that he had been attacked by two men. The first news of the murder of Henry Gage was in the Sunday morning newspapers, which were on the street early on Saturday evening. Lovey had returned to Philadelphia on Saturday afternoon, and the first news she got was a telephone call from Polly Goodbody. "Are you alone? Can you talk?" said Polly.

"I'm alone, having dinner by myself. Why?"

"Then you haven't heard about Henry?"

"Henry Gage?" said Lovey.

"He's been murdered. When did you last see him," said Polly.

"He dropped me at the St. Regis, but I had a feeling he was on his way to Harlem," said Lovey.

"You sure you didn't go with him?"

"Of course I'm sure. How was he murdered?" said Lovey.

"He was beaten and stabbed. They found his body— some kids found it under a bridge, in Harlem. The police said he'd been stabbed and beaten somewhere else, but they didn't know where. It's horrible, horrible! To think that Henry was at my house last night, dancing, enjoying life. Giggles is distraught. You must have been the last of his friends to see him alive—at least if he left you and went to Harlem. The only papers we've seen are the *News* and the *Mirror*, but a lot of people must read them. Our phone's been ringing incessantly. People can hardly believe it. I admit I wasn't very fond of Henry, but to think that this could happen to—well, he was a friend. He had certain habits that were bound to get him in trouble, but here are two detectives who want to question us. I must hang up."

It was a long time since Lovey had been talking with Grafton Williams. It was a long time since she had been to her hairdresser, since she had been having lunch at the Bellevue with Grace Wells, taken the three o'clock for New York, checked in at the St. Regis, bathed and dressed for Polly's party. The party itself had taken a long time, partly because it had been such fun. For no known reason Monroe Hackley stood out in her recollections of the party. He had danced with her twice, but so had others, and then she recalled that he had a daughter at Miss Brandon's and hating it. That was the kind of thing you talked to Monroe Hackley about, and remembered him for. She remembered a man called Alfred Eaton whom she rather liked because he always said something nice about her father. "He hardly knew me," Eaton would say. "But I liked his style." She remembered a young man named Charley Bond, who came to parties like this in the hope of being invited to play the trumpet, and brought his own mouthpiece. She remembered the Markhams, brother and sister, who danced every dance together, and were tiny, and the Shotwells, husband and wife, who danced every dance together and were tall. It was the kind of party she and Sky would never give—a nice party, and fun—but it would be remembered as the prelude to the murder of Henry Gage instead of being forgotten as the Goodbodys' coming-out party for Lovey Childs. *There were some people that things happen to and I seem to be one of them,* Lovey told herself. On an impulse she telephoned Grafton Williams, but he was not expected home before midnight; was there a message? "It'll keep," said Lovey.

Two policemen, one of whom Lovey knew, called at the house the next morning. The sergeant, Lovey's acquaintance, said, "New York wanted me to ask you a couple questions. They said you were with Mr. Henry Gage about four o'clock yesterday morning."

"Yes, about four. He dropped me at my hotel. The St. Regis, on Fifty-fifth Street. He brought me home from a party."

"At the home of a Mrs. Goodbody. Would that be the Mrs. Goodbody has the house over in Chestnut Hill?"

"Mr. and Mrs. Goodbody, yes," said Lovey.

"They spend a lot of time in New York, don't they?"

"Wouldn't you, if you had the chance?" said Lovey.

"Well, when I was younger I would have but not now no more," said the sergeant. "This Mr. Gage, he left you at the St. Regis Hotel and then he went on his way. Is that right?"

"That's right," said Lovey. "He didn't even come inside the hotel. I got my key from the night clerk and went upstairs to bed."

"That ought to be easy to check. I hate to bother you with all this, Mrs. Childs, but New York wanted to know," said the sergeant. "I hear this place is on the market."

"Yes. Are you interested?" said Lovey.

"It's a little too big for me, but I always liked the place," said the sergeant. "Don't worry about me coming here to question you, Mrs. Childs."

"I'm not," said Lovey.

"I mean, we know our people here on the Main Line. They'll have the guy that killed this Mr. Gage, or they'll give it the tear-up. There's things about this case that make me believe they'll give it the tear-up. They'll ask a few questions, then they'll sweep it under the rug. A man like this Mr. Gage, he should have known what to expect, if you know what I mean."

"Yes, I think I do," said Lovey.

"He should have known what to expect, going to

Harlem at that hour of the morning. Well, thanks for your cooperation, Mrs. Childs. I had to do it because New York asked me to, you understand?"

"It was no trouble, Sergeant," said Lovey.

She spent a good deal of the rest of the day discussing the murder of Henry Gage with readers of the *New York Herald Tribune*, but on Monday the affair belonged to the past, to the past week and therefore as much to the past as though it had occurred a year ago. Polly Goodbody, for example, did not telephone her, and since there had been so few Philadelphians at Polly's party there was no relation between Henry's untimely end and Lovey's overnight visit to New York. The Philadelphia papers carried no news of the story. Who, after all, was Henry Gage? He was a twice-divorced man who had been in the Social Register but was neither rich enough nor otherwise sufficiently prominent to merit a mention in the Philadelphia press. He did not play polo, he had not played varsity football, and his divorces were quiet.

How different it would have been if Sky Childs had been murdered, especially with the aspect of mystery surrounding the case. But nobody wondered about the death of Henry Gage, and nobody seemed to care. A man could go to Harlem, get into a jam, have his throat cut and his skull fractured, and be driven to the river's edge and his body tossed in. And what happened? The whole matter was given the "tear-up." The more she thought about that phrase, the more cold-blooded it seemed. Lovey did not have to have that bit of police argot explained to her; it was what happened to an inconspicuous man who got murdered on a Saturday morning in Harlem. And it was wrong.

She went to see Grafton Williams. "This time I'm not here to talk about real estate. It's about a murder that you may have read about," said Lovey.

"The murder of Henry Gage," said Grafton Williams.

"Yes. How did you know?"

"It's the only murder that's come into your life. I read about it in the *Tribune*, and I knew he was a friend of the Goodbodys. It doesn't seem to have attracted much attention. There's been nothing in the papers about it since the Sunday papers, and nothing at all in Philadelphia."

"And I think it's dreadful," said Lovey. She told Grafton Williams her connection with the story, and ended with the visit by the police. "Do you think they're giving it the tear-up as Sergeant McIldowney said?"

"They may be. The police don't like unsolved murders

on their books, and I have no doubt this one will be solved. But apart from that, this murder may have its messy side. Henry Gage had a brother, I gather, and he may not be too eager to have a lot of publicity about his brother's murder."

"But don't you think it's awful that a man could be murdered and nothing done about it? Even a rather worthless creature like Henry Gage. And I'm convinced that he was worthless. But he was a human being," said Lovey.

"Let's wait a week or two before forming any opinion. The police have had only three or four days to make any arrests. I don't have many dealings with police matters, but I know that a lot of their information comes from informers, or informants. Right this minute they probably have detectives working on the case."

"Well, I hope so," said Lovey.

"Why do you hope so, Lovey? What's your real interest in the murder of a man you yourself say was worthless?"

"I don't know. I'm not sure. Maybe because I was the last person in his set—how I hate that word—to see him alive," said Lovey.

"Oh, that's not bad. That's understandable," he said.

"I was afraid you were getting other ideas, suffragette ideas, I call them. My own dear wife is or was a suffragette, but she's been one since her days at Bryn Mawr. You—you don't go to New York a wastrel and come back a suffragette." He smiled.

"Still I don't have to go on being a wastrel, even if I don't turn into a suffragette," said Lovey.

"Since you know so very little about the Gage murder, I'd get some more information if I were you, before taking up the cause of humanity. Why don't you get in touch with Polly Goodbody, or Gage's brother? Find out all you can before you turn suffragette."

"I will," said Lovey.

When she got home she telephoned Polly Goodbody and was informed by the maid that Mr. and Mrs. Goodbody had left town for a few days. No, they had not gone to Philadelphia; they were just out of town for a few days. Since she was looking in the Social Register under "G," and since it had always been her intention, she looked up Gage, Adrian, whom she knew to be Henry's brother. Gage, Adrian, lived on upper Fifth Avenue; was a member of the C for Century Association and the Uv for University Club, a graduate of Brown and of the Harvard Law School, '17 at Brown and '23 at the law

school. He was married, but his children, if any, were
not old enough to be listed in the Social Register. Shortly
after seven o'clock, when she reckoned he would be
home, she telephoned him. It was answered immediately
by him, and she did not know what she was going to say.
"Mr. Gage, this is Mrs. Childs, from Philadelphia," she
began.

"Oh, yes. Is it about my brother?" said Adrian Gage.
"Where can I get in touch with you?"

It turned out that he had been wanting to talk to her,
and he was willing to come to Philadelphia any time.
The next day? Yes. He would be glad to come to her house
for lunch. No, he would not bring his wife. If Lovey
would give him directions he would drive over and be at
her house at twelve-thirty. He would need his car because he had some other errands in the Philadelphia
area.

At twelve-thirty-five he appeared at Lovey's house.
The first thing she noticed about him was he wore horn-
rimmed glasses, the second was that he drove a black
Lincoln sedan, and the third was that he wore a stiff collar.
"Very good directions," he said. "I had no trouble finding
the place." It was hard to tell whether he was younger
or older than Henry. They bore no resemblance to each

other (and as it turned out they were only half brothers, the sons of the same father with different mothers).

"It's very kind of you to let me come see you," said Adrian. "I understand you were the last to see Henry— of his friends, that is."

"I wanted very much to see you for that reason. What is the latest information you have?" said Lovey.

"The police say he went to one of several night clubs —they have it narrowed down to three or four. Any one of which could have meant trouble. I don't go to Harlem myself, never have. But apparently Henry was rather well known in certain joints. The only name for them— joints. Henry and I never had much in common, although we were friendly enough. My wife and Henry's second wife took an instant dislike to each other and we never saw them. Henry and I were half brothers, you know. The same father, obviously from the name. Henry was a son by my father's second marriage, although we were only three years apart. I don't mean to go into all this family history except to explain how different Henry and I were. My mother died when I was born, and my father married again and made a good thing of it, but naturally Henry was his mother's favorite and that made a differ- ence. For instance, I called my stepmother Mother and

Henry called her Mummy. A subtle difference, but a difference. For that reason, the closeness of Henry and his mother, and the fact that my mother was dead—I was inclined to be a loner. And of course Henry had three years at home when I was sent to boarding-school, and those are important years. I never wrote a single letter to Henry, and he never wrote to me, and his friends weren't my friends. I didn't really know Henry, if it comes to that. The girl I married was a freshman at Radcliffe when we became engaged, and I was at the Harvard Law School. I never saw anyone else until we got married. But Henry was just the opposite where girls were concerned. Henry, let's face it, was rooty. Perhaps I shouldn't have said that, but I have a feeling that you didn't know Henry very well. You weren't his type."

"Maybe not, but I came close to it," said Lovey.

"Not really. Oh, I heard about you and Schuyler Childs. I read the papers. But I don't think you were his type."

"If that's a compliment, I accept it," said Lovey. "Let's have some lunch."

Adrian Gage accompanied Lovey to the diningroom, lingering on the way to examine her father's trophies and pictures. "Your father was quite a horseman, wasn't he?"

"One of the best," said Lovey.

"Is your mother still living?"

"Yes, she's still alive," said Lovey.

"Why do you say it that way?" said Adrian Gage.

"What way?"

"I'm a lawyer, Mrs. Childs," he said. "There was something in your tone of voice."

"My mother is locked up. Incompetent," said Lovey.

"I'm sorry," he said. "We all have our troubles. Mine is my brother, yours is your mother. Is there anybody that goes through life without his share? I used to think that Henry was getting away with murder, which of course is exactly what he didn't get away with. But for years he lived the life of a ne'er-do-well, and it was as though there were no God to punish him. No justice. But I daresay that last Saturday morning, in his last few minutes alive, he paid for everything. The police say his throat was cut first and then he was bludgeoned to death. I suppose the medical examiner could tell. This isn't a very appetizing conversation."

"It's what I wanted to ask you about," said Lovey.

"Well, I'll try to spare you the gory details," he said. "As nearly as I can make out, as the police reconstruct the murder, Henry got into some altercation with two men, or even a woman and a man, during which his throat was cut with a razor. It had to be a very sharp instrument, and a razor is what they carry in Harlem. But apparently the razor didn't finish him off quickly enough, and the other person struck him on the head, to make him lose consciousness. Then they put him in a car and drove him to the river. He may even have lived a little longer in spite of the razor and the blows on the head. It was still dark. They figured that out because they dropped the body in shallow water, although a few feet away the water was much deeper. Death, by the way, was caused by drowning. Technically, Henry was drowned. They didn't have to cut his throat. The body was found by two boys who saw the body from the bridge, and they notified the police. One of the boys was a white boy, by the way. They were both about twelve years old. The colored boy's father is a policeman, and he knew what to do under the circumstances."

"What was that?" said Lovey.

"Post the white boy on the bridge so that the body wouldn't float away while the colored boy got the police."

"Have you done anything to hush up the murder?"

"Mrs. Childs, it hasn't been necessary. The newspapers took care of that by just not being interested.

Henry will go down in history as a drunk who got into a fight in Harlem. Just now people are more interested in what's going on in the stock market."

"They wrote about Sky and me, goodness knows," said Lovey.

"That's because you were rich and beautiful, and you made good reading," he said. "You lived in another world from me. Lovey Childs. Lovey and Sky."

"Well, that's all over now," said Lovey. "It was over when I got a divorce from Sky, but it was really over last Saturday morning, when Henry was murdered. That did something to me. It's too soon to say what it did, but something. Possibly a warning."

"From God?"

"Maybe from God. I haven't thought much about God," said Lovey.

"I have. I've always thought about God, probably because I was a loner all those years. Not that it did me much good to think about God. He's still as big a mystery to me as He ever was. But I like the idea of God. I even like the idea of Henry's being punished those last few minutes of his life."

"You must be out of your mind," said Lovey. "You can't mean that, Mr. Gage."

"Well, I do and I don't."

"You either do or you don't," said Lovey.

"Then I have to say I do."

"Then I'll have to ask you to leave this house," said Lovey.

"You're serious? We've just sat down to lunch."

"Mr. Gage, I've lost my appetite. Finish your lunch if you're that hungry, but you'll have to excuse me," said Lovey. She rose and put down her napkin.

"Well, I must say—what does one do in a case like this?" said Adrian Gage, getting to his feet with his napkin in his hand.

"I really don't care what you do, Mr. Gage," said Lovey. "Finish your lunch and leave."

"Oh, now really, Mrs. Childs. Because I made an unfortunate remark about Henry's being punished—I could have put it another way—"

"You said what you mean. You're one of those religious people that I have no use for. And I didn't like the way you talked with your mouth full."

"I can't help it if I'm hungry, Mrs. Childs. I'm used to talking when I eat."

"Well, I don't have to look at you, and I certainly don't have to listen. Finish your lunch, and go."

"Well, I won't have dessert."

"Have it. It's chocolate pudding," said Lovey.

"All right, I will. I might as well get a good meal out of it."

Mary, the maid, heard the interruption and took for granted that they had finished the meat course. Then when she entered and saw Lovey on her feet she asked if anything was wrong. "I'm going upstairs for a minute," said Lovely. "Serve Mr. Gage his dessert, please. I won't have any."

"No dessert, ma'am? Will I go ahead and serve the gentleman without you?" said Mary. Mary was confused.

"Do just what I said, Mary," said Lovey.

Mary took away the dishes and Adrian Gage said, "You have the help all mixed up. You ought to save your indignation for the right moment."

"I'll try to remember next time," said Lovey. She went upstairs to her room and waited fifteen minutes while Adrian Gage took his time over his chocolate pudding and getting into his black Lincoln. The maid handed her a note, which read: "Dear Mrs. Childs: Thank you for a most interesting luncheon. Sincerely, Adrian Gage." He would say luncheon.

Lovey was not made happy by the knowledge that she had made a fool of herself with Adrian Gage. His remark about being glad that Henry had been punished was horrible, but could have been passed over. It was the second time in a few days that she had misbehaved, at least by her standards: she had almost gotten fresh with Sergeant McIldowney, who fortunately had no sense of humor. Something was happening to her. Men were making her nervous, and she thought she knew why. The last person she had been to bed with was a girl, Ginny Vernon, and she wanted the next to be a man, which made her ill at ease with men. She wanted the next person, *a man*, to want her as much as Ginny Vernon had wanted her. She thought of Sky Childs, who could be made to want her from force of habit, for just the few minutes it would take. She thought very strongly and deeply of Sky Childs and of good times they had had, but she knew that after those few minutes with Sky—and even during those few minutes—she would return to the emptiness that she had known with him. Sky Childs was not the man, and besides she did not know where he was. If he came to her now, and they exchanged a minimum of words, they could have a quickie and it would be all right. But she did not want a quickie, and a quickie was all she could count on with Sky Childs before other people entered their minds. With a new person, a man, everything would be new. Even Grafton Williams would be all new. Giggles Goodbody would be all new. Henry Gage would have been all new—and it was the newness of Henry Gage that she had been toying with when she promised to go to Harlem with him. She wondered about Henry Gage and his newness and differentness. One thing was certain and that was that Sky Childs was not to be the one. There was nothing new about that cock, and nothing could make it new. But Henry Gage would have been new, and so would Grafton Williams and Giggles Goodbody and her cousin Francis Lewis and the Russian prince whose wife would not make way for an American heiress, any American heiress. Why did a Russian princess refuse to give up her Russian prince?

"This is Father McIldowney," said Grafton Williams. "Father McIldowney has been working with Austin Fitz-gibbons."

"McIldowney? Do I know your brother?" said Lovey Childs.

"The sergeant? I shouldn't be surprised if you do," said the priest. "Your house is on his beat."

"He came to see me about a murder."

"About a murder? What murder was that, Mrs. Childs? I didn't know you'd had a murder out there," said the priest.

"We didn't. It was a New York murder. The sergeant was investigating for the New York police," said Lovey.

"Actually I've known your brother for years, through my father. My father knew all the police in our neighborhood. They kept an eye out for lost dogs."

"Well, dogs are a problem out that way, I suppose," said the priest.

"They can be," said Lovey.

"Yes," said Grafton Williams. "Well, Father McIl-downey was wondering if he could go through the house from top to bottom, to make an estimate of what it would cost to convert it to a school."

"Of course. Any time, or practically any time. Do you want me to be there, Father McIldowney?" said Lovey.

"That would be very helpful if you were. It isn't absolutely necessary, but you know the house, and I understand your mother has left you in charge," said the priest.

"Mrs. Childs is in complete charge," said Grafton Williams.

"Then let's say tomorrow morning at ten?" said the priest.

"Or nine, if you'd like to make it earlier," said Lovey. "I was under the impression that priests got up at five o'clock in the morning."

"Not this priest, Mrs. Childs. Six is plenty early for me, and seven is more likely," said the priest. "I don't have a parish to look out for. I'm more in the administrative end."

"Father McIldowney looks after real estate for the archdiocese."

"Well, more or less," said the priest.

"How long would you expect to take on this tour?" said Lovey.

"Oh, four or five hours," said the priest.

"Then come for lunch, if that would be convenient," said Lovey.

"Oh, I don't want to put you to any trouble."

"It would be much more convenient for me, because I have to go to New York the next day, and we could finish up tomorrow," said Lovey.

Father McIldowney was one of the worldly breed, well tailored, with heavy silk socks, and some kind of decoration in his lapel. He resembled his brother, the sergeant, enough to show that they had the same parents, but where the sergeant looked out of uniform in uniform, the priest looked military in the black suit that fitted him perfectly. He had iron-grey hair, cut short and wavy, and he was older than his brother, but because he took better care of himself, dressed better and had the worldly air, he looked younger. Lovey somehow knew that Father McIldowney was his mother's favorite of the two brothers.

On the morning of his visit to the house he was talking to the maid when Lovey came downstairs. "I didn't know you were here, Father," said Lovey.

"You've still got ten minutes before our date," said the priest. "I have eight-fifty on the dot."

"Well, where would you like to start?" said Lovey.

"I think we can start with the cellar, if you're agreeable. These big houses always have an interesting cellar," said the priest. He asked questions about every room in the cellar—the coal bin, the wine storage, the billiard room, the cold room, the furnace room—so that it was past ten o'clock when they finished with the cellar. It was past twelve when they finished with the main floor. "I'll hate to see this ballroom stripped of all its elegance," said the priest. "But what else can be done with it? The gold leaf on the walls, for instance—it's begun to peel. The floor needs polishing. Assuming we do buy the property, the ballroom could be turned into an assembly room, an auditorium, because it's the largest room in the house and we'd get a lot of use out of it . . ."

He was thinking out loud, while Lovey's thoughts took her back to the dancing class that was held in the ballroom, to parties that her parents had given there. The actual presence of the priest, assaying the practical value of the rooms, made her realize for the first time that the house which she had not liked very much in the past was more a part of her than she knew.

"It's twenty past twelve, Father. What would you think about taking a break for lunch?" said Lovey.

"Yes, we've been at it three hours, and it must be very depressing for you, having a stranger dismantle your home this way," said the priest. "By the way, anything you want to keep, make a note of it now and I'll see that your wishes are respected.'"

"Thank you. There *are* a few things I had in mind," said Lovey. But uppermost in her mind was the fact that the priest understood what had been going on in her mind. "I suppose you're accustomed to this sort of appraisal?"

"Not with a house this size," said the priest. "And never with the owner present, with her sentimental memories. Usually I've had to inspect properties on Arch Street that weren't worth much. This house must be full of memories for you. Thank the good Lord your mother didn't have to be here."

"It's hard to say what her memories would be," said Lovey. "You know she's had a nervous breakdown."

"Mr. Williams said something to that effect," said the priest. "I'm sorry."

"Yes, I believe you are," said Lovey. "You can wash in there, and I'll be with you in a minute. Oh, would you care for a cocktail?"

"If you're having one. Otherwise, no."

"I think I'll have a dry Martini," said Lovey.

"A dry Martini would be fine with me," said the priest.

He was waiting in the den when she came downstairs. She mixed the cocktails. "I hope these are dry enough for you. Five to one was the way my father mixed them, but I notice people make them six or seven to one."

"The vermouth makes a difference. You should be able to taste the vermouth. There's something about straight gin."

"I wasn't sure whether to offer you a cocktail," said Lovey.

"Because I'm a priest? My dear lady, I start the day with a drop of wine. It isn't a Martini, but it's alcohol."

"We could have wine for lunch, if I'd only thought.

Do you know wines? I don't, but my father laid down a good supply. Shall we have a look?"

"I'm not an expert," he said.

"Well, I'm not either. Shall we just have a look? Finish these dry Martinis and we'll see what the wine cellar provides."

They returned to the wine cellar, and after considerable discussion they agreed upon a seven-year-old Chablis. "I don't recognize the name, but it should be all right," said the priest. "It should be cooled, though."

"Well, let's put it in the ice-box and have another dry Martini while we're waiting."

"Do you think we ought to?" said the priest.

"One more, and then we'll have our lunch? Okay?" said Lovey.

"Okay by me," said the priest.

They drank the second shakerful of Martinis and Mary, the maid, came in and announced that luncheon was served. "It's two o'clock, ma'am."

"Oh, why didn't you tell me?" said Lovey. "We'll be there in a minute. Go on Father, you were telling me about the Navy."

"No, I'd finished with the Navy," said the priest. "I was telling you about—well now what was I telling you about? *Rome.* When I was a student in Rome."

"That's it. Rome," said Lovey.

The priest told a story about Rome, and it was half-past two and Mary came in again. "All right, Mary, we'll be right in," said Lovey.

The priest offered her his arm and they went to the diningroom. The priest stood behind Lovey's chair, seated her, and sat down at her right. "We mustn't forget about the wine," he said.

"By no means. Mary, we'll have the wine out of the ice-box," said Lovey. "It should be cool by now."

The priest opened the wine, which they drank, and Mary served the lunch, which they rather ignored. "I wasn't really hungry, were you?" said Lovey.

"No, but the wine hit the spot," said the priest.

"Shall we have some more? Let's. It was a Chablis," said Lovey.

"It's getting on past three o'clock, and we have the whole rest of the house to see. My five hours are up."

"Screw the five hours," said Lovey. "I'm enjoying myself."

"Then let's take a look at the upstairs part of the house," said the priest.

"I don't see why not, do you?" said Lovey.

"That's what I came here for," said the priest. "I have to have a look at the house."

"Well, come on, then. We haven't got all day," said Lovey.

They went upstairs to Lovey's room, and Lovey lay down on the bed. "Just pretend I'm a nun," said Lovey.

"You shouldn't say that," said the priest.

"*I'll* pretend I'm a nun. Does that make it all right?" said Lovey. "How do I get this thing off?"

"I'll do it, it's easy when you know how," said the priest. He undid his Roman collar and was left wearing trousers and a white shirt.

"You look very different," said Lovey.

"Well, you look the same."

"Then do something about it, why don't you?" said Lovey.

"All right, I will," he said. He unbuttoned her dress and she let him slip it off. "This, I believe, is called a slip."

"You know damn well what it's called," said Lovey.

"And this is called a brazeer." He kissed her breasts.

"These are called trousers," she said. "And these are called shorts. Shall I kiss this?"

"Yes, kiss it."

"You're quite grey," she said.

"I know that. Just kiss it," he said. "Oh, that's good. I'm going to have to put it in you."

"Can't you wait?"

"No, I can't wait," he said.

"Then put it in. Put it in, quickly," said Lovey.

"It is in, you whore."

"Yes, it's in. Wait for me," said Lovey.

"I can't wait. Oh, you whore. You whore."

"That was good," said Lovey. "It was better than I thought it would be. Do you call every woman a whore, or is that because you're only used to whores?"

"I'm not used to any women," he said.

"How long has it been?"

"Months."

"Who was the last one? A nun?"

"Don't keep talking about nuns that way. I've never been with a nun."

"Why not? I've seen some pretty ones. Are you afraid they'd talk?" said Lovey.

"You wouldn't understand."

"I understood you, all right," said Lovey.

"And that's why you got me drunk," he said. He got up and put his clothes on. "You'd better get dressed too. That maid is suspicious."

"As it turned out, she has a right to be," said Lovey.

"All right, I'll get dressed. But not because I want to. I'd like you to call me a whore again. That's the first time anyone ever actually called me a whore."

"I've sobered up, and I'm sleepy."

"Father, you weren't that drunk," said Lovey. "You were a little tight, but you weren't drunk."

"What's the difference? Tight or drunk?"

"Well, I won't talk, so you're safe there."

"We'd better walk around, in case that maid is listening," he said. "I didn't like the way she looked at me. And you'd better straighten out the bed."

"Oh, I will," said Lovey. "Don't have such a guilty conscience."

"That's exactly what I do have. You don't have to care, but I do. I'm a priest."

"Then they ought to castrate you," said Lovey.

"You have a point," he said. "I was almost thirty before women began to bother me."

"That was when your hair turned grey?" said Lovey.

"Yes, how did you know?"

"I've seen your brother. He isn't grey, and he isn't half as attractive as you are," said Lovey.

"He's the one that should have been the priest, but my mother insisted that I had the true vocation. How wrong she was!"

"Did the women bother you, or did you bother the women?" said Lovey.

"Both, I guess," he said. "That was fifteen years ago, fifteen or sixteen. Let's walk around, make footsteps."

"I hope we see each other again sometime," said Lovey.

"That's impossible," he said. "In the first place, I'd have no other excuse for seeing you. In the second place, I don't want to."

"But you may want to," said Lovey.

"Then I'll have to resist temptation," he said.

"Don't resist it too strongly," said Lovey. "I could get right back into bed with you."

"So could I," he said.

"Sobering up and sleepy?" said Lovey.

"Sobering up and sleepy."

"You're a man, aren't you?" said Lovey.

"I wasn't castrated," he said. "And you're a very attractive young woman."

"Shall we go back to my room?" said Lovey.

"No, we're out of there and we'll stay out."

"Would you risk a kiss?" said Lovey.

"I would not. We'll keep walking, and what's more, I'll keep resisting. There's a side to me you don't know about, Mrs. Childs."

"Your conscience?"

"Exactly."

"But you see I don't have that, Father," said Lovey.

"I have," he said. "Let's go downstairs. In fact, it's time I left."

"Tell me, Father. Are you glad you came? You can take that either way," said Lovey.

"I won't be tonight, that's certain," he said.

She saw him to the door, where his Dodge coupe was parked.

Lovey's lust for her grey-haired priest ended two days later where it had begun—in the office of Grafton Williams. "Didn't you see the papers? You obviously didn't," said Grafton Williams. "I telephoned you this morning, but you had gone."

"I don't always read the papers," said Lovey.

"Then I'm sure you don't know about Father McIldowney," said Grafton Williams. "He was to be here this morning, but he won't be. He hanged himself."

"He what!"

"They found him in the chapel where he usually says Mass, yesterday morning. He had either just said Mass or was just about to. He was wearing his vestments, although he needed a shave, and he was hanging from a rafter in the sacristy. Nobody had seen him come or go. Well, of course nobody saw him go. I thought they usually had an altar boy to serve the Mass, but not in the chapel. It's a very small chapel and has hardly any room for a congregation, and isn't used much by the other priests for that reason. I gather it's more of a convenience for priests who want to say Mass in a hurry. It's even possible that Father McIldowney hanged himself sometime during the night. I don't suppose he said anything to you."

"No."

"The priest I talked to, a man with a Polish name, said that Father McIldowney had been working very hard lately. But he'd say that anyway. They've already issued a statement to the effect that he was overworked and under a strain. *I* didn't think he was under a strain, did you?"

"I don't know," said Lovey.

"Coming so soon after the Gage murder, this must be very upsetting to you. It's not that you knew Father McIldowney, but two things at once, so to speak. I liked Father McIldowney. I had dealt with him before, and he wasn't the usual run of priests. I always think that they're trying to convert you, and McIldowney wasn't like that at all. Well, you never know what's going on in people's minds, do you?"

"I guess not," said Lovey.

"Why don't you go for a walk and come back this afternoon, around four o'clock? Meanwhile I'll have spoken to Austin Fitzgibbons, although I doubt that he'll have anything to report on the house."

"Let's put it off till next week?" said Lovey.

She went down to the street and ran into her cousin Francis Lewis. She tried to avoid speaking to him, but he had seen her. He kissed her. "Years go by and we don't see each other, and now we see each other twice in a couple of weeks. I want to talk to you," said Francis Lewis.

"You want to talk to me?" said Lovey.

"Yes, you, if you have a minute," said Francis. "You're a cousin but you're also a friend. Let's go sit down somewhere. The Bellevue?"

"All right," said Lovey.

They took seats just inside the lobby, and Francis Lewis was purposeful. "I'm so glad to see you, Lovey," he said. "You're exactly the person I want to talk to, although I didn't realize it till just now. When I saw you at the Goodbodys' party, I thought how nice it was of Polly to put me next to you. We've always been friends, you and I, even if we don't see much of each other, and I wanted you to hear my good news."

"That you were engaged to your cousin," said Lovey.

"All but engaged, practically engaged," said Francis Lewis. "Then when the terrible news about Henry Gage became known, I must have seemed cold and heartless to everyone. But the fact was that I had some pretty bad news of my own. The day that it was in all the papers about Henry Gage, I had a letter from Rose, my cousin. It was written in India, where she was hunting tigers. And she told me that she had thought it all over very carefully and that she wasn't going to marry me. That was why she had gone so far away, to think it over, and that was what she thought."

"How sad for you, Francis," said Lovey.

"Sad isn't the word for it," he said. "I had been in love with Rose all my life, and four months ago when I asked her to marry me, we laughed because we'd always more or less taken for granted that we'd get married. There just wasn't anyone else for me, and she seemed to feel the same way. But the prospect of our getting married seemed to frighten her a little, and she put off announcing our engagement and decided on a trip to India. Whether she met someone else on her trip, or worried about the cousinly connection, I don't know. She loved me, she said, and would always love me, but not in the way two people ought to if they were going to get married. Well, that's what she went to India for, to find out, and she found out."

"I'm sorry, Francis," said Lovey. "Truly very sorry."

"Not really, of course. You didn't know Rose. And yet as soon as I saw you I wanted to confide in you. Why is that? Why should I tell you my troubles? Why was I so sure I'd find a sympathetic ear?"

"I don't know, Francis, but you have," said Lovey.

Now that was forty years ago and it hardly seems possible that Lovey Lewis has been Lovey Lewis all that time, and indeed in the memory of some Philadelphians she still remains Lovey Childs. But to most Philadelphians she has become Lovey Lewis. Not many, but still a few, can think back and recall the mild sensation she created when she married her cousin Francis Lewis. They gave it two years. "Watch Lovey," they said—and did. There was talk about her trips to New York, often without Francis. There was inevitably talk that it was Francis's money that had saved the old Lewis property and kept it from being turned into a school. In Philadelphia as the years went by it became generally known that

Francis Lewis was the quiet one and Lovey Lewis, Mrs. Francis Worthington Lewis, to give her her full name, was the animated one. And yet they became a Philadelphia team and whenever they became a team, they continued as a team, an institution. And no one knows why. Their being cousins undoubtedly had something to do with it, and their being Philadelphians had a lot to do with it; but at their twentieth wedding anniversary dinner, when old Grafton Williams was called upon for a few words, he got to his feet—with an effort, because Grafton Williams was no longer young—and said: "Why do two people such as Lovey and Francis, as unlike each other as they were, manage to stay together for twenty years? My friends, I am convinced that there's only one reason. Habit. Habit. There's no other explanation for it. That, and the fact that Lovey gave up living in New York, and they both came back to Philadelphia, where they belong."

And that was uttered twenty years ago.